Binoculars, Blue Jays, and Bloodshed

Riley Creek Cozy Mystery Series, Volume 2

Mary Lucal

Published by Mary Lucal, 2022.

Chapter One

Martha Sloane sat back on her knees, using one hand to turn her baseball hat backwards over her short brown hair. The other hand held a wet rag she'd been using to thoroughly wash every inch of the wide plank wood floor with a solution of warm water and Pine-Sol. The two rooms over Birds 'n' Beans had long been used for storage, but now they were going to serve a new purpose, and Martha had decided that a good scrub was in order. But she'd misjudged the extent to which she was *not* used to manual labor.

Surveying the rest of the floor with a sigh, she laughed. What *had* gone as she'd expected in recent weeks?

She had driven with her miniature schnauzer Penny from Boston to Riley Creek, Tennessee just a couple months ago, intent on burying her beloved Aunt Lorna, settling her aunt's affairs, and returning to her university job in the city. But the discovery of one dead body in the backyard, finding out her aunt was in near financial ruin, then coming across another dead body in the office of a used car lot can change even the best-laid plans, and *voilà*! Nearly getting killed herself in the process, Martha had helped put the murderer behind bars for life, but the financial ruin part of the story was still firmly in place, which was in part why she was scrubbing this blessed floor. She was now the owner of her aunt's coffee and birding business, Birds 'n' Beans.

Fortunately Margaret, one of her Aunt Lorna's besties and part of a group Martha now thought of as simply "the gals," was helping her with the financials for the shop. She'd quickly taught Martha that, long-term, cups of coffee and hummingbird bandanas that sold well during a single season did not a fiscally sound operation make. It was time to explore the online marketplace if the shop was to turn a steady profit year-round, so Martha had made the decision to turn the spare rooms above it into an online retail space. A night of brainstorming with some of the gals over cocoa heavily laced with Sheep Dog peanut butter whiskey produced the online shop's name: *Fly Buy Beans*.

The slightly quirky Margaret knew a good bit more than most about sales and profit margins since, much to everyone's surprise, she'd recently become a published author of steamy romance. Her keen mind for finance and her bodice ripper side gig were all the more shocking because she was so... (Martha hated the word, but couldn't come up with a better one)...*mousy*. Margaret could have been Helen Mirren's double in the film *Winchester* with her all-black getups, but she knew her way around QuickBooks like nobody's business and had gotten Lorna's financial mess sorted out over the last few weeks. Or at least, she'd helped Martha realize in a more organized way how fully submerged in the financial toilet she really was. Just like EF Hutton back in the day, when Margaret talked, Martha listened.

Aunt Lorna's passion had been for the birds: those out in the courtyard at the back of the shop; those in Bird Paradise behind her cottage; and those in the Riley Creek foothills and surrounding Great Smoky Mountains. This passion was second only to Lorna's love for her friends and customers. She'd had little time or interest for anything "on the computers," as she'd been known to say. But with barely any foot traffic trickling in after prime leaf-peeping season had passed, Martha reasoned, what did they have to lose by going online?

Oh, just thousands more dollars of advertising and packaging investments if this doesn't work, she answered herself snarkily.

Martha looked around the space and wondered again if she was doing the right thing or simply wasting her time and money on this new venture. She was still not quite comfortable with the leap of faith she'd taken. In her old university job, she'd sometimes suffered from imposter syndrome. Well, this was imposter syndrome on crack. This time she actually *was* posing as someone who knew what she was doing, when she definitely did *not* know anything about running a retail establishment.

Ugh!

Just keep on keepin' on, Aunt Lorna would always tell her. Martha had listened to that advice and, at fifty-one, had almost turned it into an art form. For years, she'd only depended on herself and her carefully crafted world: the right job making the right amount of money, and a few friends. She would never again be taken by surprise by the universe as she had been at the age of eighteen when her world was upended. Her parents had been killed in a car accident, changing completely the path she assumed her life would take. Or as she had been years later, when her fiancé Brian died suddenly and the revelations about his secret life knocked her back. It had certainly not been in her plan to deviate from her careful world...

Until a couple months ago, when events in Riley Creek had flipped everything upside down once more and made her come to the realization that what she'd been doing in Boston hardly even resembled a life well lived. So she'd uncharacteristically thrown caution to the wind and decided to make a go of it here in her beloved aunt's old home.

But now that murderous October was behind her, the reality of her situation was beginning to settle in like a big black fish crow on the end of a brittle dead branch. It was December, tourist trade had dwindled to a trickle, and money was tight. Aunt Lorna's bizarre money moves in the months leading up to her death had caused both the shop and her cottage to be sinking underwater financially, and Martha was keeping things afloat using her dwindling savings. But they wouldn't last much longer. She and the shop were badly in need of a miracle.

Shaking off her negative thoughts and forcing herself into the moment, Martha put her back into finishing cleaning the last few planks, then dropped the rag into the bucket. Just then, the trilling chirp of the belted kingfisher sounded from the shop's quirky bird clock, this particular call telling her it was 11 a.m. Penny, the salt-and-pepper miniature schnauzer who'd been curled up in her purple corduroy dog bed while Martha scrubbed, raised an eye at the sound, but didn't make a move to get up.

"What do you think, girl? Has your mom lost her everlovin' mind?" Martha interpreted the closing of the dog's eye as a probable, *yep. But what's new?*

A harsh wind buzzed the windowpane (*add installing new windows to the list of things we need and can't afford,* Martha thought), reminding her that a storm was brewing. She stood to look out, not surprised to see that the pregnant white sky of just a few hours ago had given way to a snowstorm blowing so hard, the flakes were coming down sideways. Martha's years growing up in northern Ohio and subsequently living in Boston had planted the feeling of an approaching storm in her DNA. They were in for a whopper and it wasn't going to blow over quickly. Time to wrap up the cleaning and get ready for her first Riley Creek winter.

Lucky for Martha, PJ and Helen were far ahead of her in prepping the shop for the storm. Even so, emerging from the bottom of the stairwell with Penny at her heels, she observed a scene just a hair short of frantic. On the far side of the store, Helen was battening down the "Birds" part of the business. She'd already taken down the feeders that normally hung in the back viewing garden and clustered them behind the counter. Dressed in her customary cargo pants, hiking boots, and denim shirt, she was now busily pulling breakable goldfinch mugs and ceramic wren houses from the shelves and placing them on a blanket on the floor. Martha noticed that she'd already draped a blanket over the glass cabinet holding the binoculars.

Toward the front of the shop, PJ—who had recently shared with Martha that, as she was most definitely one of the gals, she'd decided to use exclusively she/her pronouns—was rolling the three-hundred-pound Royal coffee roaster away from the front windows. Sporting a velour tracksuit, a perky ponytail, and flawlessly applied makeup, PJ was built like an oak barrel and moved the roaster like a broom across the floor. Martha was pretty sure she wouldn't even have been able to budge the hulking contraption herself. She silently gave thanks for PJ's solid muscle.

It sure got me out of trouble earlier in the fall, she thought.

PJ threw a quilted blanket over the roaster, wiped together large hands sporting rings on almost every finger, and held up her painted nails for inspection. Catching Martha watching her, she grinned and laughed a deep chuckle.

"Don't hate me because I'm beautiful," she said. Looking out the window, PJ went on, "Here it comes. I suppose all that work I did on our game plan for the tournament will be down the drain." She gestured with her chin at the whiteboard that normally held the day's lunch specials. Today, it held names of players, scoring strategies, and various other notes that PJ, as coach of the local bowling team, had made in preparation for the tournament that was only a week away. "Ah well," she said, continuing her long tradition of accentuating the positive, "we still have our shop to decorate and the holiday party to look forward to."

Yikes! thought Martha. *I still have to figure out what presents to get everyone.*

"Maybe it'll blow over and not be as bad as you think," she replied optimistically.

"Well hello, Miss Late to the Party," a voice sounded from the hallway connecting Birds 'n' Beans to Silent Sisters antique shop next door. Ethel Jean Sizemore, one of the two sisters who owned the store, came trudging in, her trademark sour expression fixed in place. "A weather emergency was issued, but I guess you wouldn't have heard it since you've been upstairs playing interior decorator."

Ethel Jean was in every way the opposite of her willowy and affable sister Mary Jane Noel, including being both short and pear-shaped. She was as practical in her dress sense as she was vicious with her verbal zingers. Her straight salt-and-pepper hair was cut close to her head—there was a rumor she cut it herself—and she wore a sensible ragg wool sweater over a turtleneck, faded jeans, and what looked to be men's fur-lined winter boots.

Two months ago, Martha would have cringed at Ethel Jean's barb. But now she knew another side to Ethel Jean, the brave and shrewd woman who had saved her from a psychotic murderess, so she let it pass.

"What's the latest?" she asked, turning to PJ.

"Don says it's already bad up in the mountains and they've closed all of the roads into the park. The National Weather Service upgraded the storm from a severe winter weather warning to a blizzard. They're saying we'll probably lose power pretty soon. Last time we had a storm this bad, the wind blew out the windows and we lost inventory, so Helen and I are trying to get things ready."

The park PJ referred to was the Great Smoky Mountains National Park. Riley Creek sat in its high foothills, just a few miles outside of its border on the Tennessee side. The little village was tricky to find, even when you knew the directions, and had spotty internet service at the best of times. In fact, it was so far off the beaten path, it didn't really get many more than "accidental" tourists, usually small numbers of nature lovers who sought out the area for camping, hiking, or birding. The result was that the residents enjoyed many of the benefits of foothills living without the crowds.

Or the customers, Martha reflected.

Because Riley Creek sat at the end of a high winding mountain road, a storm like this could easily cut it off completely. As Martha was contemplating how several days with no walk-in business would impact her bottom line, the front door was flung open. Snow whirled in and the figure entering caught the door just before it had the chance to bang back against the glass window. It was Don Chelton, Helen's husband and a ranger at Paris River State Park. He and Helen lived in the ranger cabin in the camping area, about ten miles from the national park boundary. Dressed in a parka with the state park insignia, sturdy snow boots, knitted hat and thick winter mittens, he looked every bit the outdoorsman he was.

As he closed the door on the storm, his glasses began to fog up.

"Hey, y'all, just checkin' in. It's startin' to come down bad, and we're expecting drifts and power outages. You might want to think about closin' up and getting settled in at home. Helen, you coming along soon?"

"Yep, soon as I finish moving these last pieces. I'm not taking any chances this time," Helen replied.

"OK, hon. See you back at the ranch. Just don't be too long if you can manage. We've gotta make sure the campers are squared away." With that, Don pulled his hat back down over his curly hair and turned to go.

"Hold up! Just a sec." PJ grabbed a to-go cup, walked briskly to the self-serve stations, and poured out a cup of Italian Roost. Glancing over her shoulder at Don, she said, "Help me remember. Cream, no sugar?"

"Yep, that's right," Don replied.

"There ya go. That'll keep you going in this mess." PJ handed him the cup with a cover secured on top.

"Much obliged." Don pushed the front of his winter hat up just a smidge in PJ's direction, then turned and walked back out into the swirling whiteness.

"He's a keeper," PJ said with a wink to Helen, who answered with a smile.

"Don't I know it!"

"What kind of morons would want to camp in this mess?" Ethel Jean asked with a growl. She'd sat down in a chair to watch the Birds 'n' Beans preparations, offering no assistance whatsoever. Martha tensed inwardly when Penny jumped into the gruff woman's lap, but then relaxed when she saw Ethel Jean distractedly rubbing the terrier's ears.

Helen responded as she continued to move breakables down from the shelves. "Well, there are a few diehards who like to tough it out, even though we told them about the storm as soon as we heard it might be coming our way. There aren't very many this time of year, but a handful do like to stay around to see what winter birds they might catch hanging about. They're pretty harmless and usually come prepared with plenty of campfire wood, food, and propane in case they get stuck for a few days. I sure hope that's the case this time around. Worst comes to worst, we've got an emergency generator and anyone that needs to can bunk with us." Helen turned to Martha and said, "And, Martha, you may not know this, but you have a generator out back, too."

At that moment, Mary Jane Noel came through from the antique store to stand near her much shorter sister. With perfectly styled blonde hair, she wore a pink flowing wrap over a matching turtleneck and black tights that disappeared into brown corduroy Uggs.

Fashionable, yet functional, Martha reflected. *I want to be like that when I grow up.* Mary Jane's only nod to function winning over fashion was her Timex watch. A retired nurse, she insisted on a watch with a real second hand.

"Did I hear something about closing up?" she asked lightly.

"Oh, sheesh. Figures you'd zero in on any reason *not* to have the store open," muttered Ethel Jean, gently setting Penny on the floor and trudging back through the connecting hallway her sister had just come in from. A former phone company employee, Ethel Jean was more concerned with store profits than her younger sister. While neither depended on the income from selling antiques, Ethel Jean approached running the store as if they barely had enough funds to pay their electricity bill.

"PJ, if y'all are closing up, I don't suppose you'll be selling the last of these cookies and that turtle cheesecake?" Mary Jane asked sweetly, peering longingly at the few remaining slices in the glass case next to the counter. It seemed to Martha she'd turned up her Southern twang a notch or two. Mary Jane was notorious for her sweet tooth.

"Help yourself, honey. You eat it or it'll just go to waste."

Much like any chance we might have had to bring money into the shop over the next few days, thanks to this storm, Martha thought bitterly.

Recalling the kingfisher's earlier call and guessing it was now going on 11:30, she said to PJ, "Hey, are you OK to wrap things up here, and then lock up? I promised to bring some supplies out to Albert before the storm got too bad." Albert Jeremiah, who had been her aunt's dear friend and attorney, lived alone on the outskirts of the village.

"No problem," PJ answered, waving her away with a hand. "We're just finishing up and will close things down in another fifteen minutes. Be careful going home—we don't want anything to happen to those magic hands."

In a bizarre twist of fate, Martha had filled the spot on the bowling team left vacant by the woman who'd tried to kill her in October, but she was determined not to let that little detail ruin the excitement of competing. After all, if she could survive attempted murder, she could handle a friendly little bowling tournament, right?

She donned her winter coat and backpack, leashed Penny, and out into the storm they went.

Chapter Two

Dog and human headed out to Martha's Subaru wagon parked behind the shop. Martha carried Penny over to a shoveled area to pick up the day's doggy news, but doubted there was much coming down the wire in this weather. Then she drove home to the cottage she'd inherited from her aunt and got the terrier settled in her lambswool bed in the living room.

Getting supplies to Albert will go a little easier without the young lady along, she thought. She knew the schnauzer would be mad she'd missed a trip to Albert's and that there would be hell to pay when Martha came home smelling like Penny's pal, but with the snow coming down like it was, she needed to use every moment she could. Thank goodness she had four-wheel drive. Kissing Penny on the head, locking up the house and heading back outside, she gave the car a moment to heat back up, and then hit the road.

Luckily for Martha, the two-lane road to Adair was still passable, and she reached the Piggly Wiggly just before it closed up. Shoppers were hurrying to check out with any bottled water, milk and bread that was left in stock, and Martha quickly walked the aisles and filled her own cart.

The pink-haired cashier who was scanning her items (Connie Lynn, according to her nametag) looked over her reading glasses at Martha and said, "Hey, ain't you the gal that had the trouble over t' the bird place?"

Martha, taking a moment to translate the woman's thick accent, answered breezily, "Yes, that's me. Hope it didn't give me a reputation for bad luck."

Connie shook her head in the negative. "Nah. My friend Donna used to work here and says you're top notch. She's in the senior center now over t' Evanston and says she'd *still* be on the way to her crappy son's in Florida if it wasn't for you."

"Oh gosh! Please tell her hi for me when you talk to her. I'm so happy to hear she's doing well." *Why so many flashbacks today? Can't I ever leave all that murder and mayhem behind?*

Bagging up her items in her reusable canvas bags, Martha hurried out to the car, noticing one of Connie Lynn's colleagues lock the grocery store doors behind her. Snow was beginning to make mini-drifts against the Redbox machine on the store's wall and the tires of the few remaining cars in the parking lot. She'd heard that in the south, a sure sign of Armageddon was the IHOP locking its doors. Was the Piggly Wiggly locking up a more local sign of the End of Days?

Keeping the Subaru in low gear, she drove as quickly yet carefully as she could back toward Riley Creek. The snow was driving so hard, even her wipers couldn't improve the visibility much. She took the appropriate twists and turns and finally drew up in sight of the cabin set back off of the road. To be on the safe side, she parked at the bottom of the driveway, picked up two of the shopping bags, and made her way through the snow to the front door.

Albert Jeremiah let her in and she kicked off her snowy boots. She dropped the bags in the kitchen and turned to give the elderly gentleman a hug. He was a small man (built uncannily like Tim Conway, Martha often thought) and was dressed in his customary slacks, a chamois cloth shirt and suspenders, a hand-knitted scarf around his neck a nod to the extreme cold. His house was warm—a bit too warm for Martha, still in her coat—thanks to the wood-burning stove in his study.

"We haven't had an early storm like this in quite some time," he observed. "Seems like Mother Nature just wants to remind us she's alive and kicking."

They spent a few minutes unpacking the groceries, and though he tried to talk Martha into a cup of coffee or tea, she declined.

"Albert, will you be OK here on your own?" she asked.

"Oh my, yes. Jason dropped off a load of wood for the stove last week, and now that you've brought these last few items, I should be nice and snug. I'm working on my biography of our village founder, Charlton Riley, so I have plenty of work to do." He paused for a moment. "Before you go, tell me how the online business is faring."

It took Martha a moment to recover. She'd gotten so used to being anonymous in Boston that she was still thrown by everyone knowing her business here in "the R-C," as she and her police officer pal Allison Tomlinson liked to call Riley Creek. Allison, who had become one of Martha's closest friends, was currently away at a convention in Charlotte.

"Thanks to Margaret and Joanne, it just might get off the ground once we're past this storm," she said. "I'm not totally sure how to persuade people to come to the website, but I'm working on that."

Albert nodded approvingly. "And now tell me how *you* are doing," he said softly.

For a moment, Martha's Boston sensibilities almost kicked in to produce an automatic "I'm fine," but Albert's kind eyes made her find a more honest answer. Martha had confided in him about the shocking revelations of so many weeks ago when she'd read the letter her aunt had left for her; she trusted him and owed him more than an automatic response.

"I'm doing better, Albert," she said. "Thank you for asking. Of course, I still have so many questions about everything: Aunt Lorna, Lincoln, their child... I want to know the answers to it all, but I don't know where to start, and right now I don't even have the *time* to try to find them."

Since the dramatic events of October, Martha's mind had lingered often over the fact that if Aunt Lorna's first love Lincoln and, more pertinently, their daughter were still alive, and if she could find them, she did actually have a living family member. But she and the gals had been working so hard just to keep the shop afloat that she'd had no time for anything that didn't relate to merchandising or sales.

"My dear," Albert said, "when the right time presents itself, I have no doubt you will find your way to the answers you seek. You have your aunt's tenacity."

Martha hoped silently that she would find answers to so many things in her life. The adrenalin rush of the uncharacteristically impulsive decision she'd made to stay in Riley Creek had worn off, and now reality was settling in. Had she been right to quit her job, end her apartment lease in Boston and move to the mountains? And what about Detective Perry? *Teddy,* she reminded herself. Was she really ready to explore a serious relationship? Wasn't both a new job *and* a new relationship just a bit too much?

Hugging Albert, she then slipped out the door and into the howling storm. She could barely retrace her footprints to make her way back to the wagon. It was time to get home.

The main road was even worse than it had been fifteen minutes ago, just two icy ruts she had to struggle to navigate. Reaching Riley Creek, she was relieved to finally pull into the driveway of her cottage. She carried in her own bag of groceries and was greeted by an excited Penny who, after sniffing Martha's pants, as expected gave her the canine version of the stink eye. But the little dog quickly recovered and her jumping up and down made it abundantly clear that she had to use the outdoor facilities.

Martha slid the French door to the back porch open to let Penny out, but slid it quickly closed again to keep snow from swirling in. She then retrieved an old bath towel and placed it on the floor by the door. Within a few moments, the salt-and-pepper terrier was back and ready to be let in. Penny wiggled onto the bath towel, which Martha wrapped around her just as she was about to shake snow out of her coat and onto the oak floor.

"Oh no, you don't!" Martha said, laughing as she rubbed the little dog down. Small ice balls clung to Penny's beard as Martha eased her back down onto the floor. Penny commenced smelling Martha's pant leg and looked up, cocking her head accusingly.

"I know, I know. But I just couldn't take you along this time. It's really bad out there." Her explanations didn't go very far, as evidenced by Penny walking away and plopping into her bed, head turned to the wall.

"I guess *I'm* in the doghouse," Martha mumbled to herself.

She made some easy scrambled eggs, baked beans, and toast for dinner, sitting at the farm table and looking out at the darkening night. The motion sensor lights she'd had installed came on in response to the driving snow, allowing Martha to see only about fifteen feet beyond the porch. The river rushed by another fifty feet beyond, but it was invisible in the rising storm.

Experience told her that she'd better do one round of shoveling before bed. Maybe she'd even go down the road and do the Ritzenwallers' walk, if Jimmy hadn't already gotten to it. Neighbors Jimmy and Delores were two of her Aunt Lorna's dearest friends, and Jimmy had been the one to find Martha's aunt deceased in the front yard of the cottage. Although Jimmy was retired, Delores still worked part-time at the Riley Creek Library. Martha thought of them as the closest thing she had to family, and she was grateful to be able to see their warm lights blazing when she looked out the front door's panel window and down the street.

Folding herself into her winter gear again, she added a scarf for good measure, walked down the porch stairs and to the shed in back to retrieve a snow shovel, then around to the front. As she started shoveling the wet, heavy snow, she realized that she had no salt to spread. Would Frank Elder's hardware store be open tomorrow?

As if she'd summoned him by thought alone, she spotted Frank driving his jeep slowly down the road. Distinctive with its spotlight rack, tow winch, red nose in the grill and reindeer antlers mounted from each front window, the jeep was easy to recognize even in the blizzard conditions. It drew up next to Martha's walk, the deepening snow scrunching as the thick tires came to a stop. The passenger side window rolled down and Frank's wooly-hatted head poked out, the little hair he had either side and the bald patch "up top" protected against the conditions.

Holding her mittened hand up to block the driving snow from her face, Martha greeted him.

"I'm headed to the square," he told her. "Heard on my radio that some hikers on the AT got caught in the blizzard and Don and Jason are bringing them down. They need to get them out and to somewhere warm to wait out the storm. Some VIP in the group, too, but don't know any details. Don and Jason have taken a couple of four-wheel drives over to get them at the trailhead, and I'm meeting Pastor Pat at the church to get them set up—looks like we're it. Think we could hit you up for some fresh coffee?"

Martha could barely feel her feet and her eyelashes held ice crystals, just from the short time she'd been out in the blizzard. She asked Frank to wait for her for five minutes, then quickly returned to the house. Grabbing one of Lorna's old duffel bags, she stuffed in some warm clothes and a few blankets, grabbed her keys and backpack, and with a thrown kiss to a very ticked-off Penny, was back out the door.

The AT Frank had referred to was the Appalachian Trail, the longest hiking path in the world, which stretched over two thousand miles from Georgia to Maine. The individuals who chose to hike the entire AT were called "thru-hikers." Others did it state by state or section by section, and many completed only the sections closest to home. So far, Martha had chosen this last option, hiking different parts of the seventy-some miles that stretched through Tennessee with Aunt Lorna. Though they'd never talked about doing the entire trail, it was something Martha had dreamed of as an early teen and hadn't quite taken off her bucket list.

Frank drove Martha straight to the square. Though it was now dark, the towering oaks that filled the square were visible against the night sky. In summer, they offered shady respite from the heat, but tonight, bare and black against the sky, they only intensified the darkness. Coming to a sliding stop in front of Birds 'n' Beans, Frank paused before getting out of the jeep, as did Martha. It was like they needed to brace themselves for the cold sprint to the door.

In warmer months, the shop sported several colorful yard flags with the name Birds 'n' Beans stitched across the bottom in bold letters. Sitting between Silent Sisters antique shop and Threaded Needle needlework store, it looked bleak without the customary birdhouses and birdfeeders that dangled from hangers nine months of the year. The three bistro tables with matching chairs had been placed carefully in winter storage. To Martha, the dark row of shops seemed as if they were huddling together against the cold, eyes closed and holding on till spring.

Martha showed Frank how to prep the large coffee urns while she brewed some Rufous Blend and Colombian Wing-bar, both rich enough to warm the body, but not strong enough to keep sleep away too long. Then they packed up the urns and to-go cups, and ventured out into the blizzard. Back in the jeep, Frank drove them both carefully to the First Methodist Church. He pulled up under the porte-cochère and between them, he and Martha unloaded the coffee. Then Frank stacked bags of rock ice by the door, unloaded a shovel and began clearing the area just beyond the covered entrance.

Entering the church, Martha was not surprised to see Jimmy and Delores Ritzenwaller already laying out blankets on some of the pews and setting up a table of snacks. Even at this late hour, the two octogenarians moved among the rows with an upright posture and refinement of gesture that always reminded Martha of British royalty. Both were tall and thin and dressed in simple yet quality items well suited for the weather.

"Thank you so much for coming and for bringing the coffee," came a soft voice from across the nave. Pastor Pat was dressed in his everyday clothes, and Martha had to momentarily chide herself for being surprised not to see him in his Sunday clerical robes. She had only met Pastor Pat recently, guessing from the lines around his eyes that he was about forty-five, but that was the only part of him showing any age, besides the slight limp that she knew came from a prosthetic leg courtesy of one of his three tours in Iraq. The rest of him was solid muscle. His thick neck, bulging biceps, and "high-and-tight" haircut still marked him as the Marine he'd been for twenty years.

"Of course," said Martha to the tall minister. "I'm happy to help any way I can."

"Hey, Martha!" Ellie Stephens, Pastor Pat's wife, walked up to Martha, her blonde hair pulled back into its usual ponytail. Martha had taken a liking to Ellie over the few conversations they'd had in Birds 'n' Beans, and they had a bit in common, Ellie having worked in a lab at the University of Arizona. She'd met Pat there, where they'd both been older than most of the twenty-something undergraduate students. Often, Martha wondered how they'd gotten from being students in Tucson, Arizona to minister and his wife in Riley Creek.

Now, however, Martha asked herself why Ellie looked so tired. And were those red-rimmed eyes? Had the pastor's wife been crying?

"Hey, Ellie," Martha replied. "How are you?"

Ellie smiled, but the smile didn't reach the woman's eyes. "Oh, we're hanging in there. Just concerned about this bunch we've got coming in." Martha caught the deflection, but gave into it, exchanging small talk while they waited together for the hikers and laid out blankets along the pews.

About thirty minutes later, a loud engine roared up outside the door, and then cut out. A cold, wet and tired-looking Don came through the door, followed by Martha's childhood friend, Jason Turngate, leading five bedraggled hikers. One by one they filed in, each more frozen than the last, and immediately began shedding wet clothes.

A sixth entered, distinctly different than the first five. Standing over six feet tall and sporting a dazzling white beard, he gazed around the church and smiled widely with his hands on his hips.

"Why, hello there, friends! How's this for an entrance?"

Chapter Three

How was it possible that the sixth hiker, from all appearances the oldest of the group, seemed to have so much energy? Martha watched as he shed his outer garments casually and unhurriedly where the rest of his group moved with a single goal: to get dry and warm as soon as possible. His ruddy complexion, well-toned shoulders and white beard made Martha think he might be the ghost of Ernest Hemingway, but she shook away the ridiculous thought. The rest of his group's members sat apart from one another, except for a man and woman that Martha guessed must be a couple.

"He's really something, isn't he?" asked Jason, coming alongside Martha with a steaming coffee cupped between cold-reddened hands. His ginger beard glistened with melting snow. Ellie, Delores, Frank and Jimmy were shepherding the group to the piles of dry clothes and table of warm beverages. Martha nodded to Jason and was about to speak when Don approached, his hair standing up in curly spikes all over his head.

"Radio says they're closing all the roads leading anywhere near the park. That includes ours. We were lucky to be able to get these folks down, but we're gonna be on our own for the duration."

It sounded ominous. "What exactly does that mean?" Martha asked.

"Well, the last time we were cut off like this, back in '93, the phones went first, the power second, and the radio at the police station third. Rescuers had to helicopter some folks off of the AT back then. If what we're getting is even half that bad, it'll be up to us to make it through till things open back up."

"So, how does that work?" asked Martha. "I mean, does everyone have a generator that they can use to be OK while things are off?" She was trying to take in the fact that they could be truly cut off from anything outside of Riley Creek. After all, she'd lived in Boston where nothing really closed for very long and the snowplows started salting days before the storms blew in. Being cut off there meant nothing worse than losing Netflix streaming service for a few hours and having to watch whatever you'd downloaded in advance.

"It depends," replied Jason. "Some folks depend on having wood for their fireplaces, a few have generators. Some, I'm not sure."

"But that's crazy! Don't we have a list of villagers that we check to make sure everyone is OK or something? Or don't we at least have the ability to check on our local merchants? Aren't the police doing *something*?" Realizing that she'd raised her voice and that some in the church were looking in her direction, she continued on more gently, "Please tell me *someone* is helping get everyone ready."

Jason chuckled. "Ah, Martha, always the person with the highest expectations in the room. Nah, it doesn't work like that here. Some folks live up higher toward the mountains and they don't want to be 'kept track of.' Most others, those who live in the heart of the village, expect this kind of weather might happen and plan accordingly. And the police? Well, Chief Teddy and Allison are in Charlotte, which leaves exactly three other officers. My bet is they are helping to deal with the two road closures right now. Basically, we're on our own."

An image of Shelley Duvall trapped in a snow-covered mountain lodge flashed through Martha's brain before she took up the gauntlet Jason had thrown down. "For your information, this has nothing to do with expectations. It has to do with wanting to make sure that everyone is OK. So while *some* of you are content to just sit back and let everyone fend for themselves, *I* for one think we need to check and see how people are. Starting with this bunch. Who *are* these people, by the way?" She addressed her question to Don, careful not to make eye contact with Jason.

"Funny you should ask. I should have known something was off when I first got the call to pick these folks up off the trail. Normally, the Park Service would just expect hikers to bed down in one of the AT shelters and wait out the storm. Experienced hikers know to check the weather on each leg of the trail, so they are prepared and don't put themselves or any rescuers in harm's way. Not this bunch. I got a call to get them because they weren't prepared for the blizzard and there was some muckety-muck in the group. Guess it would be bad publicity if Benjamin Marshall got hurt or died on the AT."

What? thought Martha. *Did I hear right?*

As if reading her thoughts, Jason said, "Yes, you heard right. That guy that came in last is the multi-bajillionaire owner of a private airline and booming restaurant chain, pal to Hollywood's A-listers and multiple congressmen and women. And, most recently, CEO of Big Bad Bird Tours, the world's largest eco-tourism company. That's our guest for the night."

Martha glanced over to see the bearded man, now clearly recognizable, gesturing with his long arms and talking animatedly. Looking at the faces around him, Martha could see that while one or two of the rescued hikers seemed genuinely interested, the others were just being polite. Now that Marshall was sitting down and had taken off his winter clothes, he was not as imposing as he'd appeared at first. Even though he was talkative, his posture and occasional yawn betrayed his exhaustion.

"What in the world is *he* doing up here in the middle of a blizzard?" Martha asked.

"Best we can figure, he decided to take some time off around the Christmas holiday and lead a group along a section of the AT. I heard him say something about 'needing to walk the walk if he's CEO of a company called Big Bad Bird Tours.'"

Jimmy Ritzenwaller joined them. "Unfortunately, Mr. Marshall misjudged this section of the AT in the middle of winter," he said. "According to one of the group I just talked to, they knew they were in for bad weather, but listened to Marshall who told them they'd be protected by the mountains from the worst of it. A few smart ones dropped out at the last minute and didn't join the group. This bunch is lucky you two were able to retrieve them before someone got injured... or worse." Jimmy nodded at Don and Jason, then the group fell silent for a few moments as the wind gained velocity and the icy snow drummed against the outside of the church.

"Who are the others with him?" asked Martha, gesturing with her chin at the individuals scattered around the nave. "Are they friends of his?"

"I believe the young lady with the dark hair handles Mr. Benjamin's financial affairs, the shorter man with glasses is writing his biography, the couple standing to the side are on the trip as a sort of adventure, and the silver-haired man is his personal assistant." Jimmy fell silent, as if he'd just said all there was to say. Normally, Martha found his less-is-more approach refreshing, compared to the many blowhards she'd had to put up with throughout her career. But just this once, she wished he'd been willing to pass along the facts *and* some conjecture for good measure.

Martha spotted Frank as he blew into the church, pushed by the gusting blizzard. He leaned against the door to close it behind him, and as he turned, Martha could see his eyelashes and eyebrows had iced over. She walked to the table, poured him a cup of coffee, and held it out to him once he'd removed his coat, hat and gloves, and laid them over a pew.

"Thanks," he said, taking a strong sip and wrapping both hands around the cardboard cup. "Rufous Blend. Perfect."

"How did you know it was that?" she asked, genuinely impressed with his palate.

"Simple. Medium dark roast, full body, smooth finish? Gotta be Rufous." Before she could say anything, he added, "Plus, I helped to brew it and the Wingbar back at the shop. I knew I had a fifty percent chance of being right." He smiled and smoothed down the tufts of hair on the sides of his head.

Delores joined them. "Frank," she said, "how is Hannah?" Martha knew Frank's daughter was in town at the moment, but she'd not yet had the chance to meet her.

"She's... fine, thanks for asking, Delores. She's back at the house making the most of her weak internet signal before the power goes. To be honest"—here, he paused to take a deeper swig of the now-cooler coffee—"I think she's a bit bored being here for the holidays. We don't really hold a candle to hip Asheville and I suppose she misses being with kids her own age. I mean people. Young people."

Frank continued, "Her mom, Karen, and I both thought it would be a good time for her to visit, since she has a long break from school. And gosh knows, Karen has done her time and deserves to be alone with her new husband. So I said, sure! But kids—young people—change so quickly. The bubbly teenager I remember has been replaced by an angry environmentalist who knows way more than any adult in the room. It's... challenging, let's say." He smiled almost apologetically, and Delores smiled back in an understanding way.

"Though Jimmy and I don't have children, I'm told that they are like cats. When they're little, they can't get enough of you, then they want nothing to do with you, then when you least expect it, they come back around. Perhaps she's just in that middle phase." Delores touched Frank's arm sympathetically, and then moved away.

The man with the silver haircut away from the rescued group and joined Frank and Martha. Holding out his hand, he said, "Allow me to introduce myself. My name is Dennis Tanner, Benjamin Marshall's executive assistant and general dogsbody. On behalf of our merry band, let me thank you for your care and hospitality. We are so sorry to impose on you like this, and I assure you we will be on our way just as quickly as we can. Mr. Allen"—here, he gestured at the couple—"learned on his satellite phone that the roads may stay closed for a few days, but I'm sure we'll make arrangements for transportation."

Once she and Frank had made their own introductions, Martha felt more comfortable asking some of the questions that had been on her mind.

"How did your group end up in this part of the country?" she began, trying to sound breezy while feeling insatiably curious.

Tanner smiled and said, "My dear, there are many answers to that question, depending on whom in our group you ask. Benjamin, being Benjamin, wanted to have some adventures and perfect the art of being the CEO of an eco-tourism company. He's quite enthralled with the concept of authenticity at the moment, so like any good CEO, he's made sure that *his* quest for authenticity has become a priority for those of us who work for him." Tanner shook his head. "And before you ask, part of being *authentically* outdoorsy includes having the confidence that one can guide one's peers along a well-marked trail. In normal weather, that may have been perfectly fine. In this weather, white blazes on trees didn't turn out to be quite the help he'd anticipated they'd be." Shrugging, he trailed off for a moment.

"Mr. Marshall is also an avid birder," Tanner continued, "so a secondary hope for the trip was to see some winter birds less often spotted in the New England states. He went on and on about this being an 'irruptive year' and that because some food sources—pinecones, or some such thing—are rare in the northern parts of the country, we might see unusual species this far south. He was especially hopeful of seeing a Snowy Owl. Alas, we saw what Benjamin termed 'good birds' in the days leading up to the storm, and it was probably this that kept our group on the trail longer than was eventually safe. We are sorry to have inconvenienced you all, but Benjamin is quite persistent when he thinks he may happen upon a life bird."

Clearly remembering Martha's original question, he gestured across the room at the couple. They sat close, drinking coffee and talking with one another. Martha couldn't miss the dazzling diamond wedding bands they wore.

"The Allens might give you a different perspective on the reason for this trip. They are well known within the African-American philanthropic community. Though they dabble in venture capital now, Fred came into his money working for a large telecom company, and he and Frieda actually knew Benjamin in college. They came on the trip to spend time with Benjamin and hear more about his new project. Certainly, the last project with Benjamin put them at a significant loss, and there were some hard feelings for many years. But that's venture capital: high risk, high reward. Benjamin was hoping they would put that behind them and decide to become top-level investors in his new project."

Pastor Pat and Ellie walked by, their arms piled high with pillows. They then began making pallets on various pews.

"Scott Murphy," Tanner said, gesturing at the short man with glasses who was vigorously polishing them on one of the two shirttails that hung down over his jeans, "is Mr. Marshall's official biographer, and is using this trip as an opportunity to get to know his subject better. I'm not certain he knew what he was getting into. And now, we come to the last of our happy troupe, Ana Moreno." Here he gestured at the younger of the two women in the group. Martha thought she could be a model given her striking curves, high cheekbones and beautiful, wavy dark-brown hair. As Martha studied her, Ana repeatedly tried to get cell service, holding her phone up in the air and pressing its touchscreen. From the look on her face, she was not having much luck.

"Ana is Big Bad Bird Tour's CFO and Benjamin's personal financial advisor. Right now, I suspect she is quite unhappy at not being able to check the company's market standing as of today's close of business. Benjamin convinced her that it would be good for her work-life balance to join him on this little adventure. I'm guessing she has different thoughts about that at this particular moment."

Just then, the bearded Marshall stood away from the group and raised his voice. It was deep and resonant, yet held a slight raspiness that revealed his fatigue.

"Everyone, everyone! May I have your attention?" All the people in the room hushed. "I am Benjamin Marshall and, on behalf of my group, I'd like to thank all of you for getting us down out of those mountains and safely ensconced in this warm little church. While I know we could have handled ourselves quite admirably if left to our own devices on the trail, I for one appreciate warm socks."

He laughed heartily at his own joke, and then continued. "I understand from our host Pastor Pat that we will bed down here tonight, and then revisit things in the morning. I suggest we all get some rest and let these fine villagers go home to their families. In the morning, we can figure out what to do. Of course, Pastor Pat, Ana here will more than compensate you for the use of your little manger."

Laughing, he looked around at the crowd. Ana had squeezed her eyes shut in embarrassment. Pastor Pat flushed a deep red. Martha assumed he meant Ana would sort out some financial reimbursement, but Marshall didn't seem to realize just how inappropriate his choice of words could sound to some people.

Just then, Marshall swayed a bit on his feet, and Ana darted forward to catch him by the arm before he faltered. A chair was brought and the large man sat, waving away the concerned faces that moved close to him.

"I'm all right, I'm fine," he said. "Guess the day has caught up with all of us." His face looked pale and drained even as he continued to tell those around him that he was OK.

Frank and Don offered to transport the villagers home in their snow-worthy vehicles. During the short journey, Martha noticed the tire ruts Frank's jeep had made earlier were barely visible. The snow was coming faster.

When she at last snuggled down into her bed with Penny at her feet, she did what she would always do to recharge. An extrovert according to every personality and career assessment tool she'd ever taken, she nonetheless needed the evening to herself to wind down. And the way she'd done this, since childhood, had remained the same; she reached for the mystery next to her bed. Tonight, it was one of Dana Stabenow's Kate Shugak series.

But before she could be swept into the rugged Alaskan landscape, she found herself wondering about the group huddled up in the church. She'd been on campouts and hikes before; there was something about these people that seemed distinctly different than the groups she'd been a part of.

What is it?

She lay for a moment, book in hand, trying to single out what was bothering her about the hikers. Eventually, she stumbled on it. Even though they were in a cold, exhausted state, they didn't seem connected to each other in the way that those bonded through challenge tend to be. There was no clapping each other on the back, laughter, shared relief or any of the other emotions she'd expected to see in them. If these people hadn't come on this hike at least in part to be together, why *had* they come?

Chapter Four

Early the next morning, Martha awoke to Penny burrowing deep under the covers. Usually, Her Highness slept at the foot of Martha's bed, but ended up by morning in her small flannel dog bed on the floor. At the same moment that Martha reflected on how odd it was that the little schnauzer was under the covers, she registered that her face was numb with cold. Reaching an arm out, she quickly realized the worst had happened; the power had gone out.

She lay there, not wanting to get out of her warm cocoon and hoping against hope that the power would miraculously click on. Judging by the howling wind against her window, she guessed that miracle would have to wait for another day.

She was just pulling on long johns when she heard a knock at the front door. Fumbling into her turtleneck, fleece top and corduroys, she headed down the stairs. Prancing along beside her, Penny let out an explosive schnauzer sneeze. Martha side-eyed the terrier.

"Subtle. Yes, I *know* it's freezing. Give me a minute."

Jimmy blew in the front door of the cottage, his heavy winter boots trailing snow onto the small floor rug. He held out a thermos.

"Italian Roost. You're going to need something dark and strong. Get dressed and come with me. The roads aren't great, but Frank and Don did the best they could with the plow attachments on their vehicles. I think we can get to the church with your wagon. Benjamin Marshall is missing." This uncharacteristic tumble of words coming from the tall man combined with his news to put Martha immediately on edge.

"*What*?" she said, her brain still foggy.

"Frank stopped by to tell me just a bit ago. He's asked us to come and help form a search party. Get yourself ready. Meantime, I'll dig out your wagon." Martha handed him her keys from a hook by door.

Everything is happening too fast and with too little coffee, she thought.

Jimmy turned and disappeared back out the door. Martha strapped Penny's tiny fleece coat onto her equally tiny salt-and-pepper body and opened the front door so she could go out. She knew the dog would stay with Jimmy and that there were not likely to be any passing cars to pose a danger to her this morning.

Martha slipped into her parka, boots, hat and gloves, and opened the fridge only long enough to get a splash of cream into her "Bird Nerd" travel coffee cup. She knew keeping the fridge closed was important with the power out, but this qualified as an emergency in her book. She went to the closet and grabbed her backpack, hiking sticks, and extra gloves, then hit up the kitchen for some granola bars and a Nalgene bottle filled with water. Before heading for the door, she went back to the closet and retrieved her binoculars from their peg.

She stopped in her tracks just after she stepped onto the wraparound porch and into the driving wind. The world had changed overnight. Where last night there had been about twelve inches of snow, today it looked to have doubled. Drifts had built up on the porch and against the house. She spotted Jimmy, who had shoveled the belly of the car out and was now using a broom to remove a foot-high accumulation from the top, front and rear of the Subaru wagon.

Good thing my years in Boston taught me to leave my wipers pulled out and away from the windshield. Otherwise, they'd be frozen to the glass.

She thanked Jimmy for clearing the snow, but just as she finished her sentence, he said abruptly, "You're welcome. But the snow's coming too fast. On second thought, I think we'd better take my car. Come on." Jimmy's clipped tones told Martha all she needed to know. Something serious was going on. "I hope it's OK for Penny to stay with Delores and Fritz while we head to the church," Jimmy went on, his tone slightly less abrupt, but still urgent. "The snow is really too deep for the poor girl and I already took her over to our place to get warm." Fritz was the Ritzenwallers' German Shepherd. Martha thought of him as Penny's more mature cousin.

"Of course," she replied, struggling to keep up with Jimmy as he crossed the road in the deep snow. They reached the Ritzenwallers' house and made their way to the back. Jimmy's "car" was an immaculate gunmetal-grey Land Cruiser. Raising the garage door, he opened the SUV's trunk and quickly unloaded several red plastic containers of gas. He blushed, evidently embarrassed for Martha to see that he had not taken care of this earlier.

"I picked up extra yesterday for the generator. Just didn't get around to unloading it. Let me take it to the shed and we'll be on the way." Jimmy, always efficient, had shoveled the cement path from his garage to the shed the evening before, so was quick about his task. He reversed the vehicle out, rolling down all of the windows to allow the smell of the gasoline to dissipate. Delores stood at the kitchen window with Penny in her arms, holding up the schnauzer's paw to wave goodbye.

Jimmy drove the short distance to the church, carefully aligning his tires within the two ruts that Don or Frank had managed to plow. Already snow was drifting over the lines, causing him to lean forward and squint to stay in the tracks. Martha focused on getting her coffee down in between bumps and swerves.

There were a few large trucks in the driveway of the church when they arrived, as well as Frank's familiar jeep. Frank or Don had done a decent job of clearing the lot, and huge mounds of snow were piled up here and there. And the snow kept coming.

Jimmy and Martha got out of the Cruiser, made their way through the howling wind and pushed into the church. In addition to Don and Frank, Ethel Jean, Mary Jane, Jason, Ellie and Pastor Pat were there, as well as a cherry-cheeked young policeman. Martha recognized him from a visit she'd made to the police station last fall and her cheeks blazed in embarrassment at the memory of what an ass she'd made of herself on that occasion. Given the blaze that lit up on his face when he saw her, she guessed that he remembered her too.

Carl, owner of An Early Riser bakery, and his son Lewis (whom Martha remembered preferred to go by just Lew now) were there, as well as PJ decked out in an amorphous one-piece snowsuit that gave her the unflatteringly lumpy shape of the Stay Puft Man. According to Don, Helen was back at the campground, on standby in case any of the few remaining campers had any trouble in the storm. Apparently, three women now had to weather the storm because they'd been having such fun, they had ignored the forecast snow and waited too long to break camp. Now the snow was too deep for them to tow their tiny teardrop campers home safely.

Benjamin Marshall's hiking party members were gathered in a loose group near the back of the church, each face drawn with brows furrowed. Martha quickly surmised from the various snatches of conversation that Benjamin had not been seen since they'd all bedded down for the night. Any possible footprints outside had long since been blown away by the raging wind. The group had conceded that it would be wise for them not to join in the search, given their exhaustion from the previous day's efforts. Martha heard Tanner assuring Ana that Benjamin had probably gone for a morning walk and would return any moment.

"O-OK, everyone," the police officer said hesitantly. "I've organized the search by quadrants and we'll pair up to do a grid search." He wiped his brow and Martha noted that he was perspiring heavily, even though his bulky winter coat and hat were on the table next to him. "Now," he continued, spreading out what looked like a color-coded land survey map on top of the snack table, "you'll see that I've assigned each pair a grid. Once I organize you into pairs, you will proceed to your grid. Each pair will need to return to the church every thirty minutes to check in on this log"—here, he held up a clipboard with a paper affixed to it—"and will rest for approximately thirty additional minutes. We don't want any harm to come to the rescue group."

Ethel Jean stepped forward. "No offense, Officer Organized, but by the time you get done with all of your planning and pairing and checking in, the sun'll be going down. If that geezer is outside, every minute counts." She began donning her outdoor winter clothes. "Who's ready to go?"

Martha was surprised to hear her own voice chiming in. "He's right, Ethel Jean. What's your name again, officer?" she asked, looking at the young man whose face had blushed straight down to the neckline of his flannel shirt.

"Chip," he said. "Officer Chip. I mean, Officer Daniels."

"Officer Daniels is right," said Martha. "This is dangerous weather. We have to do a search that's somewhat methodical, but still guarantees our safety. Jimmy, can you think of general areas we should search? You have the best sense of this area, given your time in Riley Creek. Everyone else, count off in ones and twos." The group quickly counted off and Martha put everyone into pairs, making sure that each pair contained one person with solid knowledge of the area. She convinced Mary Jane and Ethel Jean to stay behind in case any medical treatment was required throughout the morning. The two might have been as different as night and day, but in a pinch, Ethel Jean would be the best assistant should her retired sister need to call on her nursing training.

While the pairs assembled, PJ stood close to Martha and leaned in to whisper, "Young lady, make no bones about it. You are the person to have around in a crisis."

Martha shook off the compliment and responded, "Well, this is kind of my comfort zone, you know. Working in communications is nothing but knowing how to listen, and then bring order to chaos over and over again, just in a different flavor for each situation."

Jimmy assigned each pair a general area to search, and then everyone bundled up. Jason had brought along several walkie-talkies that were normally used by the hunting parties he guided. He distributed a handset tuned to a common channel to each pair, along with extra batteries. The pairs braced themselves with last hot drinks and snacks, and then stepped out of the warm embrace of the church and back into the roaring blizzard.

Martha was paired with Lew, and they'd been assigned the area along the road leading into the heart of the village. They trudged up the church's driveway and back out to the main road. Thinking they could cover more ground by doing so, they first decided that they would split up to walk along the tree line that edged either side of the highway, but they quickly realized that the driving snow so badly impaired visibility that they both needed to walk on the same side of the road to keep each other in sight. Martha walked on the edge of the road, watching for any signs of Marshall having passed by that way, and Lew walked along the deeper snow at the forest's edge, looking into the woods. They both yelled the missing man's name and whistled, but their words were absorbed into the driving snow.

Every ten minutes or so, PJ, who'd stayed behind with Ethel Jean and Mary Jane to manage the contact with the search team, squawked through on the walkie-talkie to get a status check. While Lew reported in, Martha took the opportunity to raise her binoculars and scan the road and woods in either direction. Just like their voices, her binoculars had limited sight in what had become a whiteout.

The pair headed back to the church after about thirty-five minutes, to rest and warm up. Then they headed out again, this time walking the main road in the opposite direction, away from the center of the village.

Around twenty minutes into their second round of searching, PJ's voice came through.

"Honey, better come back in. They've found him," she pronounced in a low voice.

"Ten-four," Lew responded. "Heading back now."

By the time she arrived at the church for the third time that day, Martha was frozen. All she could think of was getting inside, taking off her boots, and warming up her face and hands. Unfortunately, that longed-for reward had to wait a bit longer. Once she and Lew had made it back down the driveway, they saw Officer Chip Daniels getting into the driver's seat of his police-issue SUV that had been parked under the porte-cochère. Pat and Ellie, who had been paired together to search, were going into the church while Jimmy and Frank were standing close together, not yet entering. Everyone looked as frozen as Martha felt.

"Where is he? Is he OK?" Martha asked hopefully, looking around for the bearded CEO.

"Unfortunately, no," said Jimmy. "Jason and Don found him. Near the shed by the old fishing pond. He's... no longer with us."

A glance at Jimmy's expression made clear his meaning. "He's dead?" she asked. "But..." she trailed off, her already cold-flattened brain struggling to process the news.

"They're not sure," Frank interjected. "Chip is headed out there and we were just trying to decide if we should ride along."

At that, he turned to give the young officer the universal "just a sec" gesture with his gloved index finger.

"The answer is no," said Martha. "But Mary Jane should. She's the only one of us qualified to examine a body and I think it might be important to have her look at Mr. Marshall first before anyone does anything."

Jimmy and Frank exchanged glances. Frank seemed to grasp the logic of Martha's statement more quickly than the older man.

"OK," he said. "Let me make sure Mary Jane agrees to do that. Be right back." He slipped into the church. Jimmy and Martha stood for a brief time, stamping their cold feet and trying to keep circulation in their extremities.

Frank returned with two steaming cups in his hands. "She's coming in just a second," he said. "Meantime, drink this."

Martha turned to Jimmy. "You should go back in and get warmed up."

"You too," Jimmy responded as they both took a sip. "You're as frozen to the bone as I am."

"You're right. But I watched some of what happened with the two bodies back in October. I think our friend here"—she gestured at the young officer who was now resting his forehead on the steering wheel—"is going to need a hand. Plus the folks inside will need help staying calm. That's right up your alley. Keep the coffee flowing."

"Do you mean to exploit my grandfatherly presence?" Jimmy asked, waggling his brows up and down with an uncharacteristic sparkle in his eyes.

"Exactly," Martha replied.

Mary Jane and Frank, who had decided to ride along to offer what support he could, sat close together in the back of the police vehicle and Martha sat next to the young officer as he drove. His Adam's apple bobbed nervously up and down and his white knuckles grasped and un-grasped the steering wheel.

"Would you like me to drive?" Martha asked gently.

"No, thank you, ma'am," he replied, voice cracking on the last syllable. "Police code explicitly forbids civilians from driving police-issued vehicles. It's probably not even a good idea for me to have you in the vehicle, but under the circumstances, I suppose the chief would say it's OK." He swallowed hard. Martha noticed that he came to a complete stop at each stop sign they came to, even though there were no other vehicles in sight and none likely to be out any time soon.

After bumping down the icy road and making all the appropriate full stops, Officer Daniels came to the pull-off that led to the pond, and brought the car to a halt. Faint foot impressions led down the road, enough to form a path to follow as they trudged through snow over their knees. A few minutes later, they emerged near the pond. Don and Jason were standing next to a corn crib that had been on the verge of collapse back when Martha was a kid and now was not much more than a lean-to on its last legs. The pond was really just a natural indentation about five hundred yards wide, currently frozen and covered with snow. In the summer, this was fishing hole, swimming hole, and make-out spot.

Not so much today, Martha thought.

As the four drew closer, Officer Daniels called out, "Where is Mr. Marshall?"

Jason pointed down in a diagonal direction about five feet away from him. As they approached and followed his pointing finger with their eyes, Martha's stomach lurched. Benjamin Marshall was there, all right. The tips of his boots peeked out of the fresh snow, the only blemishes breaking the smooth surface of the whitened ground. About six feet to the left of those two points, a human face lay like a rounded sandbar in a placid white sea. An iced-over beard, glassy blue skin, a gash of red, staring eyes.

Eye, Martha corrected herself. Something hungry appeared to have found Benjamin Marshall before they had.

Chapter Five

No one moved except Officer Daniels, who ran behind the corn crib and said goodbye to that morning's coffee and Danish.

Mary Jane took impressive command of the situation. "OK, everyone, let's move back several feet." Collectively numb, they all took three steps back. Officer Daniels rejoined them, wiping the back of his glove across his mouth. He mumbled something that was probably "Sorry," but was lost in the blowing wind.

Martha stepped up to the young man and grasped him by the tops of his arms. "Officer Daniels, is there anyone we can reach?"

The young man was visibly shaken, but he squeezed his eyes together, and then opened them again, focusing. He raised his voice to be heard above the gale.

"Well, since Detective Perry was made Chief, he and Officer Allison went to Charlotte to some kind of police leadership convention. Last I heard, they were probably going to be stuck there for a few days thanks to this same weather system. We're just a small force and the two sergeants went down to help the highway patrol and the fire department with closing the main highways. I'm the newest officer, so I was left here to watch the station."

Wiping his nose, he continued miserably, "Shortly after that, we lost the phones, then the internet and the satellite connection, then the station radio. My best bet is the two sergeants are either holed up at the highway patrol headquarters or working accident after accident. Before they left, they told me not to worry, that nothing big ever happens here." With this, he crossed his arms tightly across his chest. "If our crappy generator works, I might be able to call out to let someone know we've got a situation, but I don't know if they'll receive our call. And all the roads into Riley Creek are likely closed by now."

Martha felt the thrill of crisis mode creep in. "Well then, it's up to us," she said. "Frank, take photos with your phone. They won't be great, but do your best. Mary Jane, confirm he's dead with some kind of... examination."

The entire group stared at her, five pairs of brows furrowed in confusion. Jason looked down at the frozen face and gestured with an elbow, obviously not wanting to take his hands from his pockets.

"Seems like the missing eye and frozen stiff body would make that pretty darn official."

Officer Daniels was coming back to life. "But... this could be a crime scene," he said to Martha. "I need to secure the body and the scene. You can't trample all over it to take pictures and such."

Mary Jane put her hand on his arm and said softly, "Officer Daniels, Martha is right. We have to make sure Mr. Marshall is deceased, and the only way for me to do that is to approach the body. And then we'll need to... put him somewhere until you have more assistance."

The young man's eyes darted around the scene, looking to be measuring his options. Then he nodded to Mary Jane.

Jason's snarky comment of a moment ago had focused Martha's brain better than a shot of house-made espresso. Looking at him, she said, "Like Mary Jane said, we do have to announce the time of his death at least, even if some birds tried to make it obvious for us."

Don chimed in, "Probably crows. Crows'll eat meat, grains, pretty much anything. They're very opportunistic birds, so any soft flesh they found on Mr. Marshall..." He trailed off, seeing all eyes on him. Martha knew it was Don's shock speaking, and she knew the others knew too.

Mary Jane stepped in quickly. "I can take some notes right now that will help with time of death. Martha's right. That will be important once a real coroner can take a look at him. Frank, take photos as I go. We're going to have to move him to bring his body back to town. You'll need to take photos of the whole process and the area surrounding his body."

As Mary Jane and Frank worked, Officer Daniels stumbled back to the SUV to get a tarp to wrap the body. Everyone else was careful to stand back and away from the scene, and they began to exchange questions with one another.

What happened to Marshall?

Had he somehow gotten lost in the dark?

Why would he have left the church in the middle of the night?

They were coming up with no answers when their conjectures were interrupted by the chirp of the walkie-talkie. It was Jimmy this time, calling to speak to Jason. Jason grabbed the handset, then walked away from the group to have some privacy. When he walked back, he was visibly shaken.

"A tree on the green just collapsed under the weight of the ice. It fell straight into my shop. Jimmy's on the way with his Land Cruiser to get me and head back to town."

It took Mary Jane another thirty minutes to "process the scene," as television crime dramas would have called it. Once Frank had finished taking photos, Mary Jane slowly began to dig Marshall out of the snow. Oddly, he wore no gloves or hat, and his flannel shirt was fully unbuttoned, exposing silvery chest hair. A Patagonia fleece, which he must have been wearing at some point, lay frozen and crumpled under his body.

Why would he have taken off his gloves, hat and coat? Compounding the strange scene was a pair of high-end binoculars, strap still around Marshall's neck and body, clutched in both of his clawed red hands. *Who would need binoculars in the dark?* Martha thought fleetingly.

Don and Frank maneuvered the frozen body onto the tarp and Mary Jane gently placed the black fleece atop Marshall's legs. Wrapping the tarp closed and grasping either end, Frank and Officer Daniels began the difficult walk back to the SUV while Don supported the middle of the grisly burden. Jimmy had already picked up Jason and they'd headed off for town to see to his damaged shop.

"He needs to be taken to the RCPD station," Mary Jane said to Martha as the two women walked behind.

"Sure, I guess so, but we need to keep him cold somehow, don't we?" asked Martha.

Mary Jane snapped uncharacteristically impatiently, "I don't care if you bury him in a snowdrift right in front of the police station, but somehow, his body needs to be secured."

Martha stopped, looking at the other woman in incomprehension. "What are you talking about?"

Mary Jane stepped closer and said directly into Martha's ear so that she would be heard over the wind, "He was shot. It was hard to see and what little blood there was had frozen into his black fleece, but I'm sure of it. He was definitely shot in the back."

In the SUV, Mary Jane shared her shocking discovery with the others and, on the way back to the church, the group came up with a strategy. Officer Daniels needed to try to raise someone more senior on the radio and satellite phone, while Mary Jane would oversee the storing of the body somewhere safe. Frank agreed to help Mary Jane, and then he'd leave to check on his daughter. Officer Daniels dropped Don and Martha off at the church; he had agreed that as a park officer, Don should notify Marshall's group of his death. Martha noted that the young officer had begun to take control. His initial reaction had suggested he was no use in a crisis, but now it seemed his training was clicking in and he held his own as they developed their plan. They all agreed that, at least for the time being, no one would tell the group at the church that Marshall had likely been murdered.

Entering the church, Martha and Don gave themselves a moment to take off their layers and get some hot fluids down. Then Don, in an official-sounding voice, notified the shocked group of stranded hikers what they'd found. The Allens held on to each other, Frieda beginning to cry. Scott Murphy sat down, a stunned expression on his face. Dennis Tanner paused, looked down, then calmly walked to Ana Moreno. He spoke quietly to her; she turned away, appearing something close to furious, and walked off. Tanner was left looking at his hands.

Wonder what that was all about, Martha said to herself.

Over the next few minutes, each person in the hiking party—apart from Tanner, who was sitting quietly in a pew—approached Ana. Martha noticed the sympathetic looks and gentle touches they gave her. Then she walked over to where Tanner was sitting and asked him if he was all right.

"I'm OK," he said. "Just in shock, like everyone else." He gestured with his chin in Ana's direction. "I can't imagine what she's feeling right now." Martha sent him a questioning look, and he explained. "I told you she was his CFO and financial advisor, because that's how she wishes to be introduced. She is also Benjamin's daughter, a fact that I believe has always given her mixed feelings."

Martha was stunned. Recovering after a moment, she asked, "But why did she get so angry just now? I don't mean to pry, but I couldn't miss what happened between the two of you."

"Because I reminded her that, immediately upon Benjamin's passing, she automatically assumes control of all his corporate interests. It was not received well."

Martha reflected on what a strange thing that was to say to someone who had just lost her father. Her ruminations were interrupted by Don's voice asking for everyone's attention again. He explained that, under the circumstances, it might be best if the hikers moved closer to town until the storm let up and additional law enforcement could arrive.

Good job, Don. Get us back to the plan.

"Surely we won't be here long," insisted Fred Allen, his arm still around his wife. His voice was an octave higher than it had been. "Surely someone will come to get us now that this has happened?"

Pat spoke up, his deep voice assuming an air of clerical authority. "Sir, I know this is an upsetting situation. But Mother Nature does what she does, and as the authorities have closed the roads down below, that means we'll just have to wait out the storm. We need to remain patient and keep our wits about us. You and your wife are welcome to join Ellie and me in our home. We have a generator and will be happy to host you as long as needed."

Next to speak was Carl, characteristically brief. "Mr. Murphy can come to us." The generator that ran the ovens in the bakery also heated the family's apartment upstairs. Murphy was still pale and clearly struggling to process the shocking news about Marshall, but he managed a weak nod without looking directly at Carl or Lew.

"We'd love to host someone normally, but with the weather as it is, I think Helen and I had better sit this one out in case any of the campers need to bunk with us," Don said, apologetically.

PJ stepped forward. "Ethel Jean will be more than happy to host Mr. Tanner and I will welcome Ms. Moreno. Isn't that right, Ethel Jean?" PJ turned to look at her, shooting her a glance that didn't invite disagreement.

Ethel Jean replied in a saccharine voice, "Why, sure, why not? I bought a three-thousand-dollar generator *specifically* so that I could host strangers caught unprepared in a blizzard."

While the hikers packed up their items, the villagers focused on tidying up the food, drinks and pallets. Martha quickly gathered together all of the "host families" (as she'd started to think of them in her own head) and issued a warning.

"We need to keep an eye open, folks. It's not clear what happened to Marshall, but there was some evidence of foul play. See what you can pick up, but also be careful. Don't assume anything about your guests." Ethel Jean mumbled something unflattering under her breath about Jessica Fletcher and a "Cabot Cove full of rejects," but PJ elbowed her into silence.

Martha continued, "Each of you is close enough to the center of town that whomever you are hosting can move around a bit. Let's all keep an eye out so we can gather information for Officer Daniels. I'm sure he'll be investigating what happened... to the extent that he can." There were glances all around, each one casting some doubt on the young man's ability to look into the foul play and remain at the police station, calling his colleagues for help.

Lew cleared his throat and said, "Is anyone else thinking what I'm thinking? Another murder in Riley Creek isn't exactly going to drive the tourists to us, is it?"

The young man had voiced what Martha herself had been thinking, but had been too ashamed to admit until the crisis of the moment had begun to wane. Her business was barely surviving as it was. If word got out that Marshall had been murdered, what would that mean for Riley Creek?

Don spoke up next. "Martha, Officer Daniels is a great young man, but he's got his hands full with the body and trying to get us connected to the outside. Do you think you could help him a bit?"

PJ nodded, starting to dress for the outdoors once again. "You *do* specialize in bringing order to chaos, honey. And the last thing any of us needs is for Riley Creek to get a reputation as Murder Town, USA."

Martha was thoughtful for a moment. Her struggling shop didn't need that either.

"OK," she said, "but quietly. I'll just keep my ears open and see what I can sort out. Everyone take your charges home and get them comfortable. Make sure you have a walkie-talkie. I'll head to the shop to see what I can get organized."

The group disbanded, divvying up into the few blizzard-worthy vehicles that were left in the parking lot. The snow was beginning to drift over the road again as they drove the short distance back toward town. Most everyone lived within a few blocks of the village green, with Ellie and Pat living the furthest away, but still in walking distance.

Martha returned to town with Carl and Lew. As Carl turned onto the road that ringed the square, they all exclaimed at what they saw: one of the oaks that had stood proudly in the center of the square had fallen straight down onto the roof of Fins to Fur, the outdoor store Jason owned. A track had been plowed all the way around the square, but the snow was too high for parking, so Carl dropped Lew and Martha off. Martha couldn't help glancing across the square to make sure no other shops had suffered a similar fate.

Jason and Jimmy had already cleared away large amounts of debris and there were neat piles of branches on the sidewalk. Jason had his Buff pulled up on his face and held a chainsaw in his leather-gloved hands. He was staring up at the massive tree. The trunk looked to be ten feet around.

Jimmy spoke in an exhausted voice. "Son, I think we've done all we can do for now. That thing is too big for us to cut down. You need professionals for the rest, or we could do more damage." Ironically, though the windows had shattered from the impact and the roof was clearly damaged, the giant tree looked at peace, almost as if it had lain down for a nap on top of the shop.

"Jason, I'm so sorry," Martha said. "What can I do?" Jason's face, what little she could see above the covering, was bright red from exertion and the biting cold.

"Jimmy's right," he said in a resigned voice. "I think we've done all we can do. I just have to board up the front windows and hope for the best once the storm passes." Martha could only imagine all that was racing through his mind: inventory, insurance, bills... and, of course, how soon he'd be able to get his business back up and running. "I've got a hunting group due up in the New Year. Guess I may have to call them and cancel."

Carl had parked behind An Early Riser and made his way across the snowy square. He had his hands in his armpits and shook his head.

"I dropped our guest off at home and Cat is getting him settled. Lew and I will help you board up the windows. Jimmy, it's going to be dark soon. You should head home to Delores." Martha was a bit surprised when Jimmy didn't object and turned for home. She left the men to their window work and headed to her own shop. The least she could do was brew up some Viennese Melody, the perfect coffee for a serious situation. So far, this blizzard had blown in nothing but bad tidings.

Chapter Six

As soon as Martha entered the shop, she knew she had a problem. It was ice cold and the lights didn't work. The previous morning, when Frank had brought her over to get coffee to take to the church, she hadn't noticed any temperature drop. Had it just been adrenalin?

She recalled being told that the shop had a generator. "Yesss!" she said aloud, mentally thumping her chest. *I am a strong, independent woman, and I have a generator!* Helen had mentioned the gizmo being in back of the shop, so Martha went directly to the back door and opened it. Luckily, an alley ran behind her shop and the neighboring businesses, and because it offered some shelter, there was only a minor drift of snow to contend with.

She spotted a covered square about two feet high and guessed that was the generator. All the times she'd hauled trash bags out to the dumpster and passed the thing, she'd assumed it belonged to one of her merchant neighbors. Unveiling it and shaking the snow off of the cover, she inspected the machine. It reminded her of a car engine, more compact but just as confusing. A thick extension cord lay coiled on the top. She searched for the "ON" button. Finding it, she flipped it. Nothing happened.

Oh great, she thought, *it doesn't work. I am a strong, independent woman, hear me freeze.* The wind was howling down the alley. She might just as well give up and go to An Early Riser to get warm, and then figure out what to do.

As she entered the back door of the shop, Frank came in the front door.

"Have you seen Hannah?" he asked urgently, not bothering to greet her. The concern on Frank's face was obvious.

"No. What's wrong?" Martha asked.

"She's taken the snowmobile out again and hasn't come back. She didn't leave a note."

"Frank, take it easy. I'm sure she just took it out for a spin. She'll be back," said Martha. "What do you mean by 'again'?"

"Yeah, you're probably right. Kids don't realize this is no weather to go gallivanting around in. I heard her start it up last night and leave, but I don't know what time she came in. I was beat from keeping the shop open late—so many people buying supplies, ya' know?—and fell asleep after I heard her drive off." He pulled a bandana from his pocket and wiped his face. His frozen hair had begun to melt and send drops down his cheeks. "Hey, it's freezing in here. Haven't you started the generator?"

Clearing her throat, Martha said in a commanding voice she barely recognized, "Well, I was just in the process of that, but I needed to come back in and put on a coat and gloves."

Frank looked at her a bit dubiously and said, "Want a hand? It won't take a sec."

"Sure, that'd be great, if you have the time," she responded, grateful that she wouldn't have to confess that she hadn't the slightest idea how to start a generator. She added this skill to the many others that had eluded her since she'd only lived in apartments with in-building handymen all of her years in Boston.

They walked back outside together. Frank knelt down, opened what Martha saw now was a gas cap, and peeked inside. Screwing the lid back on, he opened another smaller cap lower down on the machine—"Oil," he said over his shoulder—peeked in and closed it again. "Fuel line," he flipped a small white lever down. "Choke," he pulled a silver toggle to the right. "On button." Reaching to turn the red button Martha had tried, he saw it was already set to ON. Frank glanced in her direction, Martha thought with a hint of a grin. "Pull." He stood up and pulled what looked to Martha like a lawnmower cord that had been retracted inside the machine, which rumbled on with the second pull.

Frank toggled the choke lever back to the center, then plugged one end of the extension cord into the machine. He uncoiled the long cord, running it all the way back to the store. There he flipped up a metal flap that exposed an electrical receptacle. He plugged the cord in and lights flooded the shop. The HVAC unit began humming, and Martha could feel the movement of warm air from the ceiling vents.

"You're in business," Frank said, wiping his hands on his snow pants.

"Thank you so much, Frank," said Martha. "Can you stay long enough for me to brew some coffee?"

"Thanks, but I'd better keep trying to find Hannah. It'll be getting dark soon."

As Frank went back out into the snow, Martha set to brewing Rufous Blend and Sumatran Migration. She found more large urns and filled them to the top. Frank was right; the sun was dimming outside, but there were a few lights on around the square.

Jason came in the front door, juggling several pairs of snowshoes in his arms. "Hey," he called out to her.

"Hey," she said. "Can I make you a cup?"

"Absolutely." He laid the snowshoes in a neat pile over in the corner and sat down at the nearest table, looking positively exhausted. Martha could see flecks of sawdust in his beard and hair. "It feels great in here," he said, peeling his gloves off. His hands were red as steamed crabs and he flexed them open and closed. She passed him a mug and he wrapped his hands around it.

"Be careful, you'll burn yourself!" Martha exclaimed.

"Don't worry, I can barely feel it," he said, putting his cold face into the steam to warm up.

"What are the snowshoes for?" asked Martha.

"Well, I figured people might want to use them for the next bit of the bad weather. Better than just boots, they give you more surface area so you're able to walk on top of the snow instead of sinking in. My clients swear by them when we're deer hunting in January."

"Ugh." Martha made a face.

"You're as bad as your Aunt Lorna," Jason said, giving his head a shake. "Hunting is as natural as fire. In fact, humans were hunting before they invented fire. And they've been using snowshoes for more than three thousand years. I'm just continuing our human traditions, and you know I never let anyone bag more than their legal limit. Just wait till you try my venison stew." He bunched his fingers at his pursed lips, made a kissing sound, and flung his hand out in the universal symbol for something tasty.

They sat in silence for a few minutes, enjoying the feel of the heat blowing from the vents.

"So, Martha, I need to ask you a favor," Jason said with unusual seriousness.

"What is it?" It felt totally out of character for the independent outdoorsman to ask anyone for anything, and Martha felt instantly on guard.

"Well, I have no idea how soon I'll be able to get my store up and running again. Dealing with the insurance and repairs will no doubt be a nightmare of epic proportions." Martha nodded. Each day that ticked by without customers impacted all of the shop owners in Riley Creek. And not in a good way. Martha couldn't imagine what additional weeks without custom could mean to her own business.

"See, the thing is, I've been living in my back room. When I first moved in, I got the shop ready, but never got around to fixing up the upstairs. I lived at Dad's for a while, but once he got so bad I had to move him to the care facility, I started staying at the shop. As business picked up, I just stayed there on a camp cot. Eventually, I closed up Dad's house and had the utilities turned off."

"Why haven't you sold the house?" Martha asked.

"Dad is convinced he's coming home. We both know he'll never be able to be on his own again, but I just haven't gotten up the guts to tell him it's time to sell. Anyway, with the power out and the tree leaning into the shop, I was wondering... is there any way I could stay with you? Just for a while."

Martha was taken aback, but she knew Jason well enough to know what it had cost him to ask for her help. "Sure, sure, of course," she said. 'You're welcome to stay in the spare room at the cottage." Just then, she remembered. "Oh crap, Jason, I'm so sorry. The power's out at the cottage too. Penny is with Delores for now since they have a generator."

"We could... stay here together, couldn't we? I have a camp bed," said Jason quietly. Martha flinched internally, but then imagined the toasty sensation of another warm body next to hers.

Haven't felt that in a while, she thought.

"Well, I suppose I can't let you sleep in your frozen store," she said. "We could share a camp bed here till the storm blows over. It's probably a good idea for me to stay at the shop to keep the coffee flowing anyway."

"Share? Oh, uh, I wasn't asking to do that. I've got bunches of camp beds in my stock at the store. I can bring two over."

Martha's face blazed red hot. "Yeah, um, sure, that would be the way to go," she said, trying to recover herself. "Go ahead and set one up in each of the upstairs rooms." She thought quickly. "On one condition. I've got to talk to the members of the hiking group, to gather info for Officer Daniels since he's too busy managing the emergency to conduct any kind of investigation at the moment. If you promise to give me any information you hear, you can stay."

Jason looked down, deep in thought for about ten seconds. "Deal," he said with a wide grin. "I'll agree to sleep with you in exchange for information."

Martha pursed her lips, but decided not to take the bait.

"But I have one condition too," Jason added.

"Oh? And what's *that*?"

"That you stay out of this whole murder thing," he said. "Lew told me what Mary Jane discovered when she examined

Mr. Marshall and that you've agreed to look into things. I'm not entirely sure what that means, but I don't like the sound of it one bit. Recall what happened when you first came back to Riley Creek? How your curiosity almost literally got you killed?"

"Oh, please. First off, it's not up to you to tell me what to get involved in. And second, I'm only going to keep my ears open. No involvement," Martha promised solemnly, the fingers of one hand crossed behind her back.

As if on cue, the bird clock above the shop door hit three o'clock and the eastern towhee sounded its customary "Drink Your TEA!" call. Without a word to Jason, Martha finished refilling the coffee urns, and then stood at the front window, taking a look at the square. Most of the shops were closed and dark, and she assumed that folks were staying home and safe. Scanning down the block, she saw the flicker of a candle in the window of the apartment above Octavius Bennett's bookshop, Toad in a Hole. Jason had left, she assumed to fetch his camp beds and a few essentials, so she bundled up, picked up one of the urns and, pausing at the pile of snowshoes, decided to give them a try. She took a pair outside and put them on, their hook-and-loop bindings clipping her boots easily to the frames.

Upon walking, she immediately felt what Jason had described. Instead of stepping deep down into the piling snow, she walked along atop the frozen drifts, which made her trip to the bookshop much easier than she'd anticipated. Apart from the driving wind, which made even the brief walk require exertion.

Reaching the door at the back of the shop that she knew led up to Octavius's apartment, she rang the bell and waited. It was several seconds before she realized the doorbell wouldn't work without electricity, so she commenced knocking soundly until he appeared and opened the door. Comb-over perfectly in place, he was dressed in his usual argyle sweater vest, khaki pants and New Balance tennis shoes, his glasses hanging from a string around his neck. She hadn't intended on doing more than dropping off the coffee, but he invited her up for tea.

"Margaret is staying with me too, just until the power goes back on. I know she'll want to see you," he said encouragingly. Still stinging with embarrassment from her conversation with Jason, Martha decided against making a smart remark, even if only to herself, about the temporary living arrangements of the two elderly people. Instead, she gave in and removed the snow-shoes.

Reaching the second floor, Martha was pleased to find Octavius's woodstove crackling and the small living room toasty warm. Margaret was sitting in a chair close to the stove with a sheaf of papers and a pen in her hand. Dressed in a black turtleneck sweater with black knit fingerless gloves, she sported a headlamp which she switched off so as not to shine it directly in Martha's eyes. While Octavius went to fix tea, Martha joined Margaret and brought her up to speed on the day's tragic events.

"Octavius and I sensed something had gone amiss, but we didn't feel either of us would be a tremendous help. This kind of weather calls for brawn above brains. I feel a bit guilty to say this now that you've told us what's happened, but we've been editing some chapters of my next book."

Martha assured her that there were many ways to get through a storm, and that Margaret and Octavius would have had no way of knowing what was happening.

When Octavius returned with tea, he explained how much he appreciated Jason bringing him a camp stove to use to heat water. Apparently, Jason had explained how to use the device safely inside the small kitchen and left them with several packets of dehydrated backpacking meals.

"Such a nice young man," he proclaimed, and then asked about Jason's store. The two senior citizens had seen the damage from the front window, but as Margaret had hinted, they knew they could be of no help in the cleanup. Martha told them what she knew, and then changed the subject.

"Actually, I'm glad the two of you are here together. You've each been in Riley Creek for some time, so know the village merchants better than I do. I think we need to account for each person and make sure they are OK. So far, I can think of Silent Sisters, Fins to Fur, you here at Toad in a Hole, the Threaded Needle, Frank's hardware store, An Early Riser, and Looking Sharp. I can vouch for Ethel Jean and Mary Jane, Jason, Frank, and Carl and his family. But what about Carolyn from Threaded Needle, Tara from Looking Sharp, and also Alexis? I know she's moving Ohm Mama from Adair to one of the empty shops across the square here in Riley Creek. Oh, and Clint the barber. Do you have any idea of their whereabouts?"

Margaret sat forward. Taking off her kitty-cat glasses and looking serious, she ticked the names off on her fingers.

"Clint drove Joanne to Nashville since he was planning to spend a few days there too. I think they're also driving back together. I know Carolyn from Threaded Needle is still in Florida taking care of her mother after her hip replacement, but I'm not sure when she's due back. Alexis takes over the yoga studio from the bank soon, but she told Lew she wasn't moving into the apartment on the top floor until after the New Year and is spending the holidays with her family near Raleigh. That leaves Tara. Octavius, do you know anything about Tara? Did she have plans to close the shop and leave for the holidays?"

Octavius put a finger over his mouth and pondered this question. "Margaret, do you know, I *don't* know. I've been so busy with holiday stock at the store, I'm afraid I haven't been out and about as much as usual. And I don't have a personal phone number for her, even if we *did* have phone service."

Martha nodded, concerned. "I haven't really had a chance to get to know her with trying to get the online shop up and going, but I'll ask around. We need to figure out some kind of system for the merchants to check on each other in case of emergency. I'm sure she's somewhere waiting out the storm." This last she said more to ease the older people's minds than because she believed it herself.

Saying her goodbyes, satisfied that Margaret and Octavius were safe and sound, Martha walked down the stairs. Octavius, always the gentleman, insisted on seeing her out. As they reached the bottom of the stairs, he thanked her again for the coffee.

From the bookshop, Martha made the short walk to the cottage to retrieve her overnight bag, then went across the street to check on the Ritzenwallers and retrieve Penny. The side-driving snow made the walk back to Birds 'n' Beans harder than the one to Toad in a Hole, and holding Penny cuddled in her parka added yet another wriggly challenge, but nonetheless, Martha made it to the shop. When she entered, she left her iced-over snowshoes on the wide mat to melt.

"Hello there, Martha," said Carl, his deep voice still holding a hint of his native German accent. "I hope you don't mind us entering the shop without you here. I brought you some cinnamon rolls."

Sitting next to Carl was Scott Murphy. Still wearing his thick tortoiseshell glasses (*They are too large for his face*, thought Martha fleetingly), he looked up at her pleadingly.

"Isn't there any way to call out?" he asked. "I need to let my wife know I'm OK."

"I'm so sorry, Mr. Murphy, but I can assure you there's not. Even Officer Daniels hasn't been able to call out to let anyone know about Mr. Marshall's passing. The emergency folks are doing all they can, but with a storm this large, we just have to wait until it blows over and we get a phone or radio signal back."

I also don't really want anyone sharing with the world what's happened here until we can figure out what did *happen*, she reflected. *The less publicity the better, for the moment.*

Carl looked at her and raised his brows, as if beseeching Martha to help him deal with the desperate man.

"Neither of you understand," Murphy continued. "I *have* to get out of here. Benjamin Marshall's death is big news. And I have a chance to..." His last sentence trailed off, as if he was hearing himself for the first time. Martha tilted her head and looked at him.

"Mr. Murphy, are you concerned about your wife worrying, or are you...?" She had dealt with enough reporters in her life. Now that she was paying more attention, she could practically smell Murphy's wish for an exclusive story. "Pardon me for saying it, but Mr. Marshall hasn't even been dead for twenty-four hours. We don't have any idea what happened, we have individuals we need to take care of, emergency personnel are out risking their lives, and you want to cash in on a *scoop*?"

"Please, please, call me Scott. And I know—I know you think I'm horrible. It's just that I really need the money and Benjamin is past caring."

Carl raised his brows as he looked over at Martha. "If this man is one of Marshall's friends," he said slowly, "I would hate to meet his enemies."

Chapter Seven

Luckily, the electricity had not been off long enough to let anything inside the shop's industrial refrigerator get warm, so Martha was able to make the two men a simple dinner. Enjoying ham sandwiches and potato salad, they ate with an unspoken agreement to talk about anything but their present situation. Martha peeked out the front window from time to time, hoping against hope that the storm would subside and they could get back to normal. The rising and falling wind had begun to set her teeth on edge, and the fact that Benjamin Marshall had been murdered added an additional chill.

The sun had gone down; it was going on six o'clock. Martha was gathering their dishes when something out on the square caught her eye. Putting the dishes down on the counter, she squinted out the shop's front window and saw someone had shoveled the community firepit out, as well as cleared a large space around it. Four people were scurrying to add wood to the small fire, huddling close to it for warmth when they weren't busy feeding it.

Carl, Scott and Martha bundled into their outerwear and headed out to join them. Within a few paces, they recognized Pastor Pat, Ellie, and the Allens.

"What are you doing?" Scott called to them above the wind.

"Making a bonfire, in honor of Benjamin," Fred Allen replied, feeding the fire with small logs from a nearby pile. Frank had joined and was busying himself by gathering and adding more downed branches to it.

"The pastor and his wife have been very hospitable, but we couldn't stay in the house any longer. We just needed to *do* something," Fred said.

Pastor Pat glanced at Martha apologetically. "It's not uncommon that, in the wake of the loss of a loved one, individuals wish to memorialize that person in some way. The Allens asked if they could come into the square, and when I saw all the limbs stacked up from the tree that fell on Jason's shop, it just clicked in my mind that a fire could be a fitting memorial—perhaps the only memorial for now—for Mr. Marshall. I hope it's all right."

Martha looked off into the blinding snow and saw the candle flickering in Octavius Bennett's window. The exhaustion of the day caught up with her and she was momentarily reminded of the enormity of the storm, the crushing finality of a life lost, all that she had lost so recently herself. She held her hands out to the flames. The blaze had now taken hold and the fire grew high and strong.

"Of course it's all right," she said. "Even in the midst of a crisis, we have to mark the passing of friends and family."

As they stood together, all gazing into the fire, Martha pointed to Birds 'n' Beans and explained to the Allens that she was the shop's owner. Then she said to Mr. Allen, "I don't mean to sound intrusive, but I'm not totally clear how you and your wife knew Mr. Marshall. Mr. Tanner mentioned when we were at the church that you were thinking of investing in a new venture that Mr. Marshall had in mind, but I don't know much more."

"First off, please call me Fred. Frieda and I don't much stand on ceremony. Oh, Benjamin and I go way back. To Harvard Business School, as a matter of fact. We were in the same cohort back in the late '70s. We were going to change the world, one dollar at a time. I went to work for a large telecom company around the advent of the first PC. Those were the days! I started at the bottom, but we'd all gotten stock deals, and the more the company grew, the more it sold parts of the business, bought new lines, so all the time our personal shares were increasing in value."

He paused to use the toe of his boot to adjust a log that had fallen to the edge of the firepit.

"Eventually, this son of a small engine repairman was moving up the ranks and in charge of over two hundred employees. I was making more money than I thought I'd ever have in one lifetime. Frieda and I had gotten married and had two sons by then, but we had lost touch with Benjamin. Not out of any personal enmity, but just because, as they say, 'Life happened.'

"Fast forward a few years and he calls me out of the blue, inviting me to come back to Cambridge for a reunion of our cohort. Really, it was just a grandiose cocktail party where everyone shared their successes and networks, but it was actually a great weekend. A few weeks later, he calls and asks if I'd have any interest in investing in a company he was starting. Frieda and I had never invested in anything like that, but by then we'd saved enough money to fund the boys' college, pay off our house, and plan for a pretty great retirement. With some left over, you know?

"He pitched an idea about a windfarm up in Maine. At first, I thought he'd lost his mind. But the more I thought about it, the more it resonated with me. I wanted to leave more of a legacy than shares of stock, you know? The rest is history. I've come along with Benjamin when he's had a project focused on sustainability, and we've almost always gotten our initial investment back, and then some."

"Sounds like you two had a great friendship. But, if you don't mind me asking, why were you on the AT with Mr. Marshall? Was it just a vacation for you?" Martha took in Fred's Patagonia parka, hat, and gloves, and ventured a guess that his winter boots cost five times more than hers.

Fred seemed to follow her line of thought. "I know, I know. What's an office guy like me doing in the backcountry? Well, we were actually along so that Benjamin could pitch his latest idea to us. He wanted to talk about the project 'in context,' as he said, while we hiked through America's longest trail. Something that, in his words, 'awakens the very spirit of exploration.'"

Frieda cut in. Martha guessed the attractive woman was accustomed to helping Fred come to the point.

"This one was about birds, saving the birds. We basically came all the way up here in the snow, so Benjamin could see some winter birds."

Scott Murphy jumped abruptly into the conversation. "But it was so much more than that, Frieda! Surely you can see that? He was creating something no one had ever imagined before. He was taking that dusty, ancient building full of papers that he'd bought on a whim years ago and transforming it into a research facility for the future. He was moving it from a money pit to a financial engine, capitalizing on international collaborations with the chance to win external funding support."

Scott spoke with the conviction of a zealot, his voice booming above the ever-present wind, and Martha had to remind herself that he was talking about a research facility for birds, not a matter of national defense. She felt thoroughly confused, but before she could start on the string of questions she had on the tip of her tongue, another voice rang out in the darkness. It was Dennis Tanner, walking purposefully toward the ring of light emanating from the steady fire. Ethel Jean followed behind him, her opinion of being out in the cold announced by her deep frown.

"Ancient building full of papers? Far from it, Scott, and you know it. The Stedman Library has been cultivated for years, through generations and generations of gifts and careful stewardship, to become one of the preeminent holdings of rare books in the western hemisphere. It protects and conserves the papers of some of the finest writers of the early Americas. There are living authors of the highest order who only *dream* of being able to leave their manuscripts to the Stedman. We've had first editions of our civilization's greatest books pass through our doors, some of the earliest maps ever made. Why, even some illuminated manuscripts are kept there, available to the world's scholars."

"Blah, blah, blah." Ethel Jean was the Silent Sister who could keep silent no more. "I'm freezing my tuckus off out here. Maybe we could save this love affair with birds and books till morning? All you Boy Scouts can have another little campfire when the blizzard dies down. Hell, I'll even throw in a bag of marshmallows."

Martha couldn't help herself. "I have so many questions and I can ask them tomorrow, certainly, but what is an illuminated manuscript?"

"They are books that were often handwritten on animal skin." Tanner had taken on a pedantic tone, as if he was a professor at the front of a class. "Some dating from as long ago as the 1100s, they were often inscribed with gold or silver. They are incredibly rare and only studied and handled by a very small number of individuals."

Fred chimed in. "That's what Benjamin wanted to pitch to me. See, he said there were several other collections that would be delighted to take some of the Stedman works and continue their care, precisely *because* the items are so rare. Benjamin had a serious love of just about anything that had to do with birds and their conservancy, so he wanted to build a state-of-the-art bird research center. From what little he did tell me, he was talking *big*. He had plans to buy the properties on either side of the Stedman and use that land as part of the project as well. We're talking something that, in size, would rival the Smithsonian museums in Washington."

Tanner's eyes flared. "And anyone worth their salt would know that a collection like the one held by the Stedman cannot simply be broken up and shipped off. It was the collection itself—those items that, together, comprised such a unique research opportunity—that made the Stedman. Why, as a young student, I came across a book with notes in the margins and—lo and behold—those notes turned out to have been written by Mark Twain. That book now sits in the Stedman as part of a not-insignificant collection of Twain's papers. I *knew*

Benjamin. He would never have gone through with breaking up the collection. It is too important."

Ana and PJ had arrived at the circle. Martha was astounded. Every single person in the group of hikers had, one by one, made it to the village green and to the fire.

"A celebration of life, here in this tiny mountain town? How fitting. How quaint. My father would love the notion that he'll be written about as dying among the 'common man.'"

Martha was stunned by the acidity of Ana's words.

"You knew my father, Dennis?" the young woman went on. "Oh *really*? If so, I hope you'll help Scott finish his book so I can read all about him." With this, she brought a flask out of her pocket, took a deep swig, and sent it around the circle. Most of the hikers partook. "I'm sure it'll be a bestseller, unlike some of your other so-called biographies."

Martha registered that Ana didn't seem quite as steady on her feet as she'd originally been. She looked over at PJ, her expression wordlessly saying, *"Really?"* PJ shrugged the shoulders of her parka lightly, looking sheepish, and edged around the circle to Martha.

"I'm sorry. What can I say? The poor girl began drinking as soon as I got her settled in at my house. She had a bottle of something in her bag. I didn't realize how much she'd had. She wanted to come to the square just to get out of the house and we saw all of you here at the bonfire. The vibe isn't quite what I'd expected, but in my experience, sometimes people need to blow off steam to get through a tough situation. Let me see if we can't channel it just a bit."

Clearing her throat, PJ addressed the group, letting her powerful voice boom out over the wind. "Since we are all gathered here together, may I suggest you use the power of the fire as a means of celebrating the recently departed Mr. Marshall? It's obvious he wasn't perfect. But I ask you, which of us is? Surely there was something about him that each of you cared enough about that you'd spend the days right before the holiday hiking in the cold with him. Perhaps each of you could say a few kind words about him as a way of marking his passing today."

"Come on," Ethel Jean said grumpily to the circle. "Say your one thing so I can get my butt home and into my warm bed."

Fred was the first to contribute. "Benjamin loved big ideas, ideas that would change the world. Most people were afraid to think on that scale. To Benjamin and his big ideas."

Scott was next. "Benjamin wanted his success to be mine. He wanted to lift others up. To a wonderful mentor. You shall be missed."

Frieda added, "Benjamin's birding tours brought visibility to endangered species all around the world. To Benjamin, for using his fame for good."

Tanner spoke more sincerely than Martha had heard him yet. "Benjamin embodied the concept that with great privilege comes great responsibility. He used that privilege to share knowledge with others. To Benjamin."

It was painfully poignant that Ana was the last of the hiking group to speak. Taking a long draw on her flask, she held it up in the air and said, with eyes watering, "To my father."

The hikers and villagers stood together around the fire, the flames lessening in intensity and the wood pile depleted. It was too late to retrieve a fresh stack, so the tribute became a solid bookend to what had been a very long day. With mumbled goodnights and a few embraces, the group broke up.

PJ leaned into Martha. "We're going to need to keep these folks occupied. Let's get them all home and into bed tonight, and I'll see what I can come up with tomorrow. But I think we just got a glimpse of what can happen if they're left with too much time on their hands."

Martha nodded. "Agreed. I'm going to work tomorrow on seeing what I can find out, but I'm also going to ask all of you hosts what you've picked up."

As Martha and Jason came together to head to the shop to turn in for the night, they hesitated when they heard the unmistakable sound of a snowmobile approaching. Frank broke away from the circle and ran across the square, waving to the driver who could barely be seen in the dark behind the machine's bright headlight. The engine cut out and Martha and Jason heard Frank and his daughter arguing, their voices carrying even in the winter gale. Thinking something might be wrong, Martha turned and headed toward them, Jason plodding through the snow behind her.

"I don't care if the guy *is* dead. Probably good riddance for the whole planet!" Hannah was standing and holding the snowmobile helmet under her arm, her brow and lip piercings glinting in the light still being given off from the fire. Her helmet-flattened Mohawk lay against her head. She wore camo pants, a puffy black parka, and army boots laced up to mid-calf.

Frank looked horrified. "Good God, Hannah, what's the matter with you? The man's friends and daughter were just gathered right here in the square not ten minutes ago to say goodbye to him, and you're saying good riddance? What's gotten into you?"

"Dad, everyone knows that the older you get, the more conservative you get. You can't see this guy for what he was. You're just blinded by the fact that he ran some major eco-tourism company that was 'bringing attention to the plight of endangered bird species'"—here she added air quotes—"But did you ever stop to think what he did to the areas where those birds lived? Did you? Well, I'll tell you. Our sustainability professor actually uses Big Bad Birds as a case study in his intro classes. Those areas went from being shrinking habitats to nearly non-existent. Once Marshall and his 'teams' went in, what came after were cameras, and then tourists trampling all over the place trying to add 'lifers' to their lists. Sure, maybe he created a tourist trinket shop or two, but the person who really benefitted was him!"

Martha opened her mouth to try to calm the situation, but Hannah plowed on. "And do you even know what else he did, in addition to tromping across the world looking for endangered birds? I'll tell you. He invested in fracking companies that force toxic chemicals down into the earth in order to get natural gas out, poisoning rivers and lakes all over the Southwest. Who knows what other pies his fingers were in?" She paused.

"Wait, actually, I know one pie his fingers were in for sure. While his first wife was living in the U.S. and he was trotting around the globe, he picked up a hot Brazilian actress and had a love child with her. That's the kind of guy Marshall was. So excuse me if I don't wail and cry and rend my garments over him.

If you ask me, the universe did itself a favor. Addition by subtraction."

With this, she threw her leg over the saddle of the snowmobile, turned the key and cranked the machine back on. "I'm going to park this in back. See you at home in a while," she yelled over the engine, and then roared away into the night.

Frank turned to Martha and Jason, obviously embarrassed. "I'm sorry," he said. "She's twenty and thinks she knows everything. But that was totally unacceptable. I'll talk to her tonight. Now I think I'll head home and get myself ready for what is sure to be a totally unpleasant conversation. Night, guys." Frank turned and headed in the direction of his shop, where he, like Octavius, lived on the second floor. Martha watched him hunch his shoulders against the cold and, likely, brace himself for the blowout he was about to have with his daughter.

"Ugh," Jason said. "That was me in my twenties. Poor Frank."

"Oh, please. Don't even remind me about me at that age. Cringe-worthy for sure," agreed Martha as they walked in the direction of the shop.

"She seems so angry," Jason observed. "But from what I heard, he and she have a pretty good relationship."

"Do Frank and Hannah's mom get along?" asked Martha. She wasn't trying to be nosey, but she'd never really been able to assemble Frank's backstory from the bits she'd heard from Mary Jane.

"From what Frank has said, they got along great, just as soon as they were no longer married. His ex—I think her name is Karen—moved back to Philly to be near her parents, but when she was a kid, Hannah visited Frank regularly. Frank and

Karen sound like two of those amazing divorced people who truly figured out how to co-parent. They even went on college visits together, the three of them. Ah well, if you figure out parent/child relationships, write a book and it'll make a mint. As for me, they'll probably remain a mystery for the rest of my days."

Entering Birds 'n' Beans, Martha made a beeline for the back door to let Penny out to browse the viewing garden. Its location had left it fairly protected so the snow was shallow enough for Penny to maneuver around in. The clock struck eight with the doleful call of the mourning dove.

How fitting, Martha thought. Gazing out at the night, she was quiet for a minute, reflecting on Jason's childhood and all that came with having an alcoholic dad who was also one of the town's most popular guys. Martha recalled the summers when she would visit Riley Creek, and Jason would try anything, *anything*, to stay out a little longer and avoid going home. She could still remember her Aunt Lorna saying, "Poor child," as she gazed at the boy with stooped shoulders heading down the street on his bike in the dark. At a young age, Martha hadn't been totally clear what it was at home that he was avoiding, but as she got older, Jason had confided in her about his parents' arguments and the physical abuse he'd endured when his father came home drunk.

No wonder he'd gone out west just as soon as he could.

Penny came in and shook the snow from her coat. Reflecting on the theme of parent/child relationships, Martha ran back over the shocking things Hannah had said to Frank about Benjamin Marshall. Even though she knew many college students held strong opinions, Hannah's statements had still seemed extreme.

But what do I know? Martha asked herself. *I'm a thousand years old compared to Hannah. Maybe I've just forgotten how college kids think. Maybe she was tired from taking the snowmobile out today as well as late last night.*

She froze in mid crouch. She'd been about to give Penny a scratch, but instead stood bolt upright.

"Jason, Frank told me Hannah had taken the snowmobile out last night. Late."

"Yep," Jason responded, "he told me too—" She saw the dawning realization in his eyes. "Ah, no," he said, shaking his head from left to right. "Surely not."

"I don't think so—I hope not—but you have to admit the timing fits. And those things she said... she really seemed to harbor a deep resentment of the guy."

"I can't think any more about this tonight," Jason said. "I've set a cot up in each room upstairs, along with a pillow and sleeping bag. I'm turning in." He held her eyes for a few minutes, then headed for the stairs.

Martha turned and gazed out one last time at the glowing embers in the square. What would Mary Jane and Frank think of her for even contemplating Hannah as a murder suspect? Still, her job was to bring order to chaos, wasn't it? Riley Creek needed this murder solved, and fast. And here was one puzzle piece that potentially fit.

Martha made her way upstairs and to her own makeshift bed. As she and Penny snuggled down on the squeaky camp cot and Martha reached for her mystery to allow her brain some respite, a final nagging question sounded in the back of her mind.

Where is Tara Jackson?

Chapter Eight

The night brought another six inches of snow, this atop the already-frozen foot or more that had fallen over the past couple days. The village square had gotten plenty of foot traffic along the single lane of street that had been plowed out the previous day, but the fresh snowfall made it look like the town was starting from scratch.

Martha had gotten up early and taken the stairs down to the shop to make fresh coffee. She knew that many in Riley Creek did not have power and that a cup or two of Brazilian Tailfeather might make all the difference to them as they endured the winter siege. Jason had gotten dressed and gone to his shop to check for any additional damage.

She had managed to brew a few urns and refill the half and half dispensers when Officer Daniels blew in on a gust of cold air.

"Morning, Officer Daniels. How are you?" Martha asked, filling a mug with steaming coffee and pushing it across the counter to the young man without asking. From the looks of him, she wasn't certain he'd changed his uniform or even slept last night.

"'Bout as good as can be expected, ma'am," he said, nodding gratefully at the cup. "I got a few hours' sleep in the cell, but stayed up trying to reach the Highway Patrol most of the night. Got only static. My guess is that the radio towers are so frozen over that nothing's getting in or out." He took a deep breath, exhaled, and pulled his winter hat off. The hair underneath stuck out in every direction, reminding Martha of just how young he was. "Oh, and please call me Chip."

"OK, Chip. What can I do to help you?" she asked in a calm voice. "And you can call me Martha, not ma'am."

The young man smiled in acknowledgement, then said, "Well, to be honest, I put any investigation of Mr. Marshall's... situation... on hold, knowing none of the hiking group could go anywhere and that you would all keep an eye on them. But without knowing how long it'll be before we get any help up here, I need to gather some information from everyone that was with Mr. Marshall the night he went missing. I don't have the proper resources—crime scene investigators, a coroner, and all that—to do it properly, but I can do some pieces myself. When Chief Perry finds out what happened, he's going to ask me for information, and I've got to have something to give him." He gnawed on a thumbnail. Martha was all too familiar with Teddy Perry's intensity when it came to investigating a crime, so she thought the young man was exactly right. Once Teddy found out there had been a murder—another murder, she corrected herself—he would want answers.

"Why don't you conduct your interviews here?" she asked the officer.

"What, here in your coffee shop?" he asked, surprised.

"I think you mean here in my coffee and bird merchandising empire," she said, sweeping her arm around the shop in an expansive gesture. "Which location do you think would put your suspects more at ease? Here or the police station?"

"Well, the station *is* only on emergency power and it's just me there, so I haven't even made coffee this morning." He paused. "You might be onto something. I guess I could close the station for just a few hours to do interviews here." But he was still a bit hesitant. Once Martha had reassured him some more, he began calling those with walkie-talkies to get the word out that the hikers' presence was being requested by Officer Daniels at Birds 'n' Beans.

Before the first hiker showed up, PJ blew in and held the door open for Hannah. They both held bakery boxes in their hands. At Martha's questioning look, PJ said, "Carl had some muffins still on hand and did a small bake early this morning. We can use the salamander to warm things up good enough to make sure everyone who wants one has something hot for breakfast. Come on, kid." At this, PJ gestured to Hannah to drop the boxes on the counter. Hannah did as PJ indicated, and then crossed her arms over her chest.

PJ went on, "Frank mentioned that this one knows her way around a coffee shop. Figured she could start earning her keep a bit by helping us get through the storm. People need to be fed and people need coffee. We're going to see that that happens." She threw a clean apron to Hannah and said, "Put that on, cranky butt, and start steaming some milk. I'm going to make sure yesterday's dishes are all done."

Hannah was visibly resentful, but did as she was told, possibly because PJ made it clear that she was not exactly making a request.

Martha showed Chip into Silent Sisters, Mary Jane and Ethel Jean's adjoining antiques shop, which would be a good place to conduct his interviews. Since the power had been out, the place was pretty cold, but he set up a table and chairs just beyond the hallway connecting the two shops. The space afforded both privacy and a draft of warm air from Birds 'n' Beans. And fresh coffee.

Martha was busily arranging the rest of the tables that, just a couple days before, had been pushed to the walls in anticipation of the windows possibly breaking when Don came in, visibly relieved by the warmth that hit him. He announced that Helen had sent him down in the campground's jeep to check on things in the village, and also to ask if the three campers who'd had to weather the storm could come to town for a bite to eat and a hot coffee.

"Of course!" Martha replied. "I'm sure the walls of their campers feel like they're closing in by now."

As Don went out the door, he held it open for Scott who headed straight for one of the tables nearest the picture windows in the rear of the shop. Looking out, Martha saw lots of birds flitting in and out of the treed courtyard where her Aunt Lorna had designed a small sitting garden several years before. Much like Bird Paradise, the backyard glade Lorna had made for the birds at her cottage, the courtyard featured multiple feeding stations: platform feeders, tube feeders, thistle bags, and suet cages.

The benches that encircled the area were now covered in snow, but that didn't stop the birds from perching on them and flying back and forth to the feeders to check for errant seed. In all of the excitement of the last couple of days, Martha hadn't refilled the feeders.

Those poor birds must be starving! she thought. *Aunt Lorna would have fed her birds before feeding these humans.*

As Martha went about getting her boots on before going out to fetch the bird food from the closed storage bin behind one of the courtyard's small crystalline-like trees, she made out Scott setting up his laptop and getting down to work. As she filled the feeders, Chip approached Scott, the two of them exchanging some rather unpleasant-looking words, and then Scott walked off with the policeman in the direction of Silent Sisters.

Martha finished filling each feeder, feeling like Tippi Hedren in Hitchcock's movie *The Birds* as the different species came whooshing in around her to partake of her offerings. *The only difference*, Martha thought with a bit of smugness, *is that Tippi had to put up with ravens and seagulls, whereas I have to contend with these ridiculous blue jays.* As usual, the flamboyant blue jays were the bullies of the playground, defending "their" feeders against smaller birds.

Martha was holding the backdoor open and clapping out her boots when Ellie and Pat came in the front of the shop accompanied by the Allens. The Allens looked confident and strangely carefree, whereas Pat's eyes darted nervously toward Ellie from time to time. Ellie's brow was creased and she once again looked like she'd been crying.

Scott emerged from the Silent Sisters hallway, looking to Martha a bit flustered. Actually, he'd seemed flustered the whole of the short time Martha had known him, so this was an entirely subjective assessment. But his face was reddened more than when she'd last seen him.

Fred and Frieda plopped down on two adjoining barstools, Fred announcing to the room, "I could die for a venti latte." At this, the low hum of conversation in the shop came to a virtual silence. Fred cleared his throat, uttering, "I'm sorry." His wife murmured understanding whispers to him, but it took a few moments before the people in the shop started talking again.

Dryly, Hannah said, "There's coffee in the urns in the self-service area. We're not doing any espresso drinks today."

"Nonsense!" boomed PJ's voice from the kitchen. "Today is a perfect day for espresso drinks." She came bounding out of the kitchen, telling Hannah, "While we have electricity, we'll be serving up whatever delectable concoction these folks are in the mood for." Hannah stared at PJ wild-eyed. "Mr. Allen, isn't it? What can we get started for you?"

"It's Fred," the man stated, looking slightly sideways at his wife and clearly being careful not to sound too excited, given the faux pas he had committed moments earlier. "And if you can do a latte, ma'am, I'd be most grateful."

PJ gave a huge grin and raised her voice. "Latte on deck! And pop a heart on top, if you will, please." Hannah deftly began to work the espresso machine, still frowning.

"This is crazy," she muttered. "I'll do a latte. Plain." But PJ ignored her, still smiling and making small talk with the Allens.

Ellie's voice sounded in Martha's ear. "I feel like Charlie in the friggin' Chocolate Factory," she hissed. "How can PJ be so cheery?"

"Oh, she's not cheery," said Martha. "She's just being PJ. You may not have spent enough time around PJ to know that she'll work like hell, even ignoring her own emotions, to make those around her feel better. And she's giving it all she's got today." Martha looked over in time to see PJ scoot Hannah out of the way with a swift swing of her ample hip so that she stood in front of the machine. In her left hand, she took the ceramic cup into which Hannah had just poured a shot of espresso. In her right, she held the metal carafe of steamed milk. Raising her hand so that the carafe was almost eight inches above the cup, she began to stream the milk into the espresso. At the last moment, she brought the milk down closer to the cup and, with a flick of the wrist, halted the pour and handed the cup to Hannah.

"Whoa!" said Hannah, looking down into the cup, a smile breaking over her face for the first time that morning. "You do latte art?"

"Oh, honey, that's the least of what I can do." PJ flipped her kitchen towel over her shoulder and strolled back into the kitchen. Hannah was left, latte in hand, mouth hanging open. She turned to Fred and placed the cup down on the counter in front of him.

"Sir, your latte. With a heart, courtesy of PJ." Fred and Frieda looked down into the cup appreciatively.

"Make that two," said Frieda.

Over the next thirty minutes, all of the hikers and their hosts had arrived. One by one, Martha observed them as they came through the front door, perking up at the warmth of the shop and the familiar scent of coffee. Each of the hosts' houses would have been comfortable enough, powered by a generator, woodstoves, or some combination of the two, but there was something elemental about the smell of brewing coffee and baked breads that Martha knew would help them face the new morning and the interviews with Officer Chip.

Satisfied that everything was running smoothly, Martha gently coaxed Ellie to a chair two tables away from the others.

It had been obvious when she'd arrived that she was on edge, and Martha wanted to find out why.

"Ellie, what's going on?" she asked, deciding to come straight to the point.

Ellie glanced over at her husband, who was holding a muffin in one hand, a cup of coffee in the other, and talking amiably with Ana Moreno and Dennis Tanner. With all of the hosts (except Ethel Jean, who was checking in on Mary Jane) and hikers present, there was a pleasant buzz of conversation going on. The only sound missing to Martha's ears was laughter, which made sense given the events of the past twenty-four hours.

"All of this. Being here. Being the minister's wife right at the time the minister needs most to minster." Martha was totally confused, so stayed quiet. This was an old tactic she'd learned to use at the college when dealing with upset board members. Simply stay quiet and eventually they'd pop. And Ellie popped.

"I know you don't know me that well. I mean, you only just got here to Riley Creek. We've been here for years. Five years. We only expected to be here for three at the most, and then we supposed the church leadership would move Pat to a new post, hopefully one closer to a big city. But there's no sign we'll be moving any time soon, and my time is running out."

Martha sat, stunned. Did Ellie have some kind of incurable disease? Ellie must have seen in Martha's eyes that she'd assumed the worst. She reached across the table and grabbed Martha's hand.

"Oh no, nothing like that. I mean, my time to have a baby is running out. My fertility."

Martha probably knew more about incurable diseases than she did pregnancy, but nodded in a way that she hoped conveyed understanding.

"I'm thirty-four, Martha. Don't you know what that means? My fertility clock is a ticking time bomb and every time I go into the city, my doctor tells me I'd better hurry up. As it is, I'll need to get shots and be close to a doctor to help us conceive. And living up here in the middle of nowhere..." She shrugged her shoulders, leaving Martha to fill in the blanks.

"But why don't you get the church to send you someplace else?" asked Martha. Not having been raised in a religious household, she had no idea how such things worked. Was there a relocation office that specialized in moving ministers? Did they own panel trucks that proclaimed on the side "Let the Spirit Move You" in big block letters?

"It doesn't work like that. The thing about Pat is that he's the ultimate peacemaker, almost to a fault. He entered the ministry to find peace after his years of active duty, and now he's just about taken that to an extreme. He doesn't really understand. He's forty-nine, but as you know, fertility isn't the same for men. We need to be somewhere where we can be close to a fertility clinic since we'll probably need to make lots of visits. With things so quiet at the moment, we'd planned to take a trip to Knoxville before the holiday season starts to see a specialist and perhaps try some new fertility drugs, but now I see how impossible that plan is going to be. If we can't be close to a doctor, we can't start this process."

By this time, Ellie had tears in her eyes, and Martha could feel the heat of the younger woman's anguish. Martha herself had never felt the urge to reproduce, she supposed due to losing her own parents so young. Her early adult life had been more about regaining her emotional equilibrium, finishing school, and achieving financial independence. Flights of fancy, including her early dreams of being a writer, had quickly made way for a much more practical version of herself. Her single-minded drive, which for women of certain ages often translated into a drive to have children, had in Martha resulted in a very successful career at a young age.

Children had never been in the equation. There was a moment they might have been, right around the time she and Brian had been talking about getting married, but after she found out that he already *had* children, and a wife he had failed to mention, it had put her off the idea and even more firmly on the career track. Her work had never let her down, she had always been in control, and she'd never felt childlessness as a void in her life. But she ached for Ellie. Every woman, she thought, could relate to wanting something so badly she could taste it, but that thing being at the same time completely out of reach.

By the time the two women wound down their conversation, three strangers had come in. Martha thought—uncharitably, she knew—that the group of women who had been left stranded in the campsite looked even more raggedy than the hiking group had when they'd first arrived at the church. All three ordered coffee and cinnamon rolls and took a seat at an open table.

Scott, who had been tapping away at his keyboard ever since his meeting with Chip, glanced up at them. Martha expected him to ignore the trio as he seemed to be ignoring everyone else, but instead he did a double take, staring at one of the women with his mouth partly open.

Just then, a sequence of events occurred in such close succession, it was as if one gave birth to the next. First, Ethel Jean banged into her shop next door. Martha could hear her raised voice through the hallway.

"Yes, I *see* you've set up a table here in the hallway, Captain Obvious, but GET IT THE HELL OUT OF MY SHOP!" Then the short salt-and-pepper-haired force of nature stalked into Birds 'n' Beans and proclaimed, "I don't care if Barney Fife here hasn't found out yet who knocked off Daddy Warbucks, I didn't invite him into my shop so he needs to stay OUT OF THERE!" With this, she turned and walked back into Silent Sisters, passing Chip who'd promptly moved his table and chairs from the antiques shop side of the hallway to the Birds 'n' Beans' side.

"Knocked him off?" Ana Moreno asked, looking from Martha to Chip and back again. "What's she talking about?" But before a red-faced Chip could recover enough to explain, Scott stood up, pointing at one of the three campers who'd recently seated themselves.

With a quavering yet passionate voice, he said, "If you're looking to arrest someone for Benjamin's murder, she's right there!"

Chapter Nine

Chip Daniels' face and ears blazed their telltale pink, and his mouth opened and closed, making him look like a fish dropped onto the sidewalk. He started to speak, then closed his mouth, then repeated the sequence.

PJ casually walked up beside the young officer and murmured, "Chip, dear, close your mouth," before continuing to move along the counter, pretending to polish it. Ana stared at Chip and repeated her earlier question.

"Is Ethel Jean saying my father was *killed*? And what are *you* talking about, Scott?" She rounded on Murphy. "How do you know these women?" She pointed in the direction of the three who'd come down from the campground.

Chip cleared his throat. "Ms. Moreno, I'm sorry to tell you like this, but yes, there appears to be a strong possibility that your father was the victim of foul play. We won't know for sure until an official postmortem is completed, but initial signs suggest he was shot."

"Initial signs like a bullet in his back," came a yell from Silent Sisters.

Hikers and campers stared in shock. Tanner struggled to speak but, appearing to change his mind, slid into a stool at the counter and stared at his hands.

"But why didn't you tell us yesterday?" Ana persisted.

Martha waded in to help the young officer. "We didn't want to jump to any conclusions, and we didn't want any of you to be more upset than you already were with the news of Mr. Marshall's death."

Tanner, who appeared to have recovered from his shock now, said acidly, "What she means to say is that they wanted to keep an eye on us, because they think one of *us* is the murderer."

Chip put both hands up in a defensive gesture. "Mr. Tanner, Like Martha said, let's not jump to any conclusions—"

"Clearly, my boy, you're having trouble *walking* to any conclusions, let alone *jumping* to them. It's high time you did your duty and got us out of this godforsaken excuse of a town and let some *real* detectives determine what happened to Benjamin," Tanner responded. Young Chip's face blazed crimson as if he'd been struck. Pastor Pat, who had been sitting at a table with the Allens, stood from his seat and walked over to be next to Chip.

"Officer Daniels is doing everything he can, ladies and gentlemen. Ellie and I have lived in Riley Creek long enough to tell you that only Mother Nature decides when it's time for us to rejoin the outside world. Until then, everyone needs to remain calm and do the best they can to cope with these difficult circumstances."

Martha was grateful for his imposing physicality and commanding voice. The clamor that had hinted at chaos immediately died down.

PJ's deep voice cut in. "OK, folks, here's the deal. Since we are going to be stuck here together for the next however many hours, we need to get busy. There's work to be done and everyone is going to chip in. Except you, Ms. Moreno, given the circumstances." PJ nodded sympathetically in Ana's direction. Pulling a small spiral notebook out of her apron pocket, she used the tip of her pen to go down a list she'd prepared sometime that morning.

"Scott, you and Jason are going to be in charge of shoveling. I suspect Don and Frank have been trying to keep the square and a few of the nearby roads somewhat cleared, but with the snow still coming down, we need you on shovel and salt patrol."

Scott protested, "But I've got work to do on my manuscript. I really can't—"

"Hey, buddy," Jason cut in, "in case you haven't noticed, a tree decided to take up residence inside my business across the square. There's nothing I'd rather do than go in there and start figuring out the damage to my inventory, but I know now's not the time. So you need to shut down the computer and get ready to work." Scott closed the lid of his laptop with the pout of a toddler being told it was bath time.

"Ladies from the campground and Hannah? You're with me on cleaning up after breakfast and figuring out dinner." Hannah predictably rolled her eyes, while the three women looked at each other, then Chip, then back to PJ. But they remained silent.

"Mr. and Mrs. Allen, I know Delores needs help at the library and I think it would be great for you to give her a hand there. We'll radio Jimmy and ask Delores to get ready for you to head down to join her." Fred Allen rubbed his hands together, seeming excited about receiving his assignment. His wife's expression remained neutral.

"I'll take Silver Spoon off your hands. I need some manual labor, after all," came the disembodied voice from Silent Sisters.

"Huh?" PJ called back, brow creased in confusion.

"Silver Spoon. The stuck-up guy. Derek, Dennis, whatever."

"Sure thing, honey." PJ nodded at Tanner, who Martha thought looked simultaneously offended and relieved to have been chosen. "He'll be on his way just as soon as he's ready, Ethel Jean!" PJ called back toward the antique shop. "Now, I want you all to go back to your hosts' homes, get cleaned up, and report to your assignments no later than two o'clock. That will give you plenty of time to make progress and meet back here for a warm dinner around 5:30."

Chip chimed in. "I'd like to see you three ladies from the campground before we call Don to come and get you, please."

"It's OK, Don let us drive his truck down so we have plenty of time," one of the women said. She and her friends walked with him toward the back of the shop and took a seat at his makeshift interview table. The hikers and their hosts donned winter coats, hats, scarves and mittens before trickling out of the shop and into the storm.

PJ walked over to Martha. "Hope that was OK?" she said.

"It was perfect," said Martha. "For a second there, I felt like we might have a mutiny on our hands."

"Well, some of the gals tease me about the movies I watch, but one thing I've learned from them is that a group of terrified people stuck in one place need something to keep their minds busy. Think *Poseidon Adventure*. Think *Armageddon*. *Towering Inferno*." PJ crossed her arms with a look of satisfaction, then used one large hand to pat her somewhat frazzled hair and added, "I like to fancy myself an aspiring Shelley Winters, you know."

Martha nodded. "Not sure I like comparing our situation to a sinking cruise ship, an asteroid about to crash into the Earth, or a skyscraper that's imploding, but I get your drift. People in a crisis need something to do." Then she cocked her head and said, "And Shelley Winters has got *nothing* on you."

Scott approached Martha to ask if it was safe to leave his laptop in the shop, and she told him yes. With one last longing gaze back at the machine, he exited with Jason to return to An Early Riser. Ana was now the only member of the hiking group in the shop. She drained her coffee cup, then got up and came over to Martha.

"Please," she said, in a voice empty of the self-confidence that she'd displayed thus far, "I know you are trying to be kind to me, but I'd like something to do too. Actually, I think I *need* something to do. I don't care if it's manual labor. I'm more than capable of doing that."

Martha understood immediately. In the days following her parents' death, Lorna had kept Martha busy with assembling and taping boxes of items for Goodwill and organizing those things she wanted to bring with her to Riley Creek. In the face of teenage Martha's objections, Lorna told her none too gently that she had to keep on keepin' on and that she'd better jump to it. Jump to it she did. And it had been that activity that had most likely saved her from falling apart those first difficult weeks.

Now she faced another woman who'd lost a parent. How could she fail to help Ana put one foot in front of the other?

"Well, sure," Martha said. "Why don't we go upstairs? I'm sure there's something up there that needs to be done."

They ascended the stairs to the rooms Martha had prepared for online orders.

"What is this?" asked Ana, taking in both rooms and the camp beds made up in each.

Martha felt herself redden. "I'm sure it will seem silly to someone as successful as you, but it's my attempt to enter the online marketing scene. My aunt left me this shop in her will and I decided to make a go of it."

"Do you have a background in sales?" Ana asked, still taking in each of the rooms.

"Well... no. My background is marketing and communication." Martha felt so self-conscious in front of the other woman, even more so when Ana pulled her hair out of its bun and it tumbled down around her shoulders in a perfect swirl of curls. Martha imagined she herself was probably sporting some hideous hat-and-bed-head hybrid.

"I'd say you have more than you need." Ana sat down on the chair in front of the computer. "I've noticed that people here seem to listen to and trust you. It's the same in any business, large or small. If people believe in you and trust your product, the rest is logistics."

"You make it sound so easy," Martha said, feeling herself relax.

"Oh, I never said it was easy, but there's a method to it, which you can see if you observe long enough."

"Did you learn your business skills from your dad, if you don't mind me asking?" Martha said gently.

"Yes and no. I learned business principles at the Yale School of Management. I learned how to put those principles to work for maximum profit while helping Benjamin with his business ventures," the young woman replied wistfully.

"Why do you call him Benjamin?"

"He and my mother had broken up before I was born. I grew up with her in Brazil, so to me, for the longest time he was like a fascinating uncle who came to visit and I called him Benjamin to sound more grown up. I would only see him every few years or so, when he visited his Brazilian holdings. It just sort of stuck.

"My mother was a popular actress, so between the two of them, they provided me with a rather affluent childhood. She was very clear that she wanted to raise me, so I think he was careful to keep his distance, but he fulfilled his responsibility as best he could."

Ana teared up and Martha waited a few minutes before asking her next question.

"Did you resent not being raised by him?" She hoped she was not being too invasive with her questions, but sensed some kind of kindred spirit in this woman.

"Growing up, no, not really. I always knew he had a wife in the United States. When he did visit, it was like a vacation. He would whisk me off to shop, play, ride horses, whatever I wanted. But after my mother died, a few years before I went to graduate school, I did become resentful in a way. Her death left me completely unanchored, even though I had lots of friends. I knew she'd insisted on raising me solo in Brazil. But why did he agree to that? Yes, I guess you could say I grew into my resentment a bit later in life."

"Well, I'm sure everyone looks back and wishes they'd done something different," Martha responded. "But as the saying goes, hindsight is 20/20. If you and he started working together after your mother's passing, I'm guessing you had time to make up for those lost years?"

"Yes and no," Ana said again. "I'm ashamed to tell you this, and you won't think much of me once I do." She paused. "I went to Yale to spite him, you see." She went on to explain to Martha the rivalry between her alma mater and her father's. "I wanted to be his opposite in some way, to hurt him for being away all of that time. Ironically, I ended up being every bit as good at business as he was. In some ways, I am much more like him than my mother.

"I graduated from Yale and began working for a corporation in São Paulo where I learned everything I could about corporate finance. Benjamin invited me to come work with him some years later, and since that time I've taken over all of his financial operations. He didn't always appreciate my methods, but I was able to help him finance his pet projects." She shook her head regretfully, the circles under her eyes darkening her olive complexion even further.

"I'm not sure I totally follow you," Martha said.

"Big Bad Birds and all of his other environmental interests are bankrolled mostly by investments that are far from socially acceptable. He didn't like it, but he couldn't deny that by investing in things like fossil fuels and fracking, I was able to earn him money for things like the Center."

"And what exactly *is* the Center?" Martha asked. "I heard some of the group talking about it at the bonfire, but I couldn't quite put all of the pieces together."

"The Moreno Center for World Bird Conservation is to be the largest single physical location bringing together scientists, researchers, and philanthropists, all focused on bird research. My father got very interested in birding some time ago. About a year ago, he came across a well-respected study that said that in the U.S. and Canada, wild birds had declined by something like thirty percent. Around three billion birds, he told me, had simply disappeared. And we're talking all kinds of birds: shorebirds, forest birds, grassland birds. It stunned him, and he suddenly wanted to do something about it.

"And what was my father best at? Bringing smart people together to make money. So he came up with the plan for the Center. He wanted to sell off or give away the Stedman's collections and demolish the building as part of a much larger footprint dedicated to the Center. Pulling together investors who would provide seed money, he felt sure if he could create a state-of-the-art facility, with the best minds connected to it, then the decline in the wild bird population could be slowed or even stopped."

"And he was going to name it after your mother?" Martha asked softly.

"No. That's the worst part." Ana's tears were coming again. "He wanted to name it after me."

"But why is that the worst part?"

"I'd spent the last several years working for Benjamin, while simultaneously resenting him. I expressed that by turning his investments toward things he didn't believe in, and I allowed him to be crucified in the public eye for it. But he never forced me to change our strategy. He told me he supported my decisions, and all the while he was torn apart by the media for being a 'two-faced environmental phony.' I'd only recently realized how selfish I was being, and I planned to make it right, but we really needed the money to fund the Center's construction, so I thought I'd wait until we were on firmer footing before changing our investment profile. Now it's too late for me to say sorry. And it's too late for me to revive him in the court of public opinion. And it gets even worse."

Martha wasn't sure what could be worse than Ana's father being murdered, but she kept that observation to herself.

"When you told us at the church that Benjamin had died, Tanner informed me that the will leaves the entire corporation and all of its holdings to me. After all I've done to him, he left me everything."

"Was that what Tanner told you that made you so angry? I kind of noticed that."

"Yes and no," the other woman responded for the third time. "You see, in some ways, Dennis and I are very much alike. We are devoted to my father's business enterprises, but for different reasons. Dennis is devoted to the Stedman and to supporting the person who created and maintained it." Martha must have looked baffled as Ana went on to explain. "Benjamin owned the Stedman collection. Did you not know?"

"No, I didn't. I guess I should have realized, but thank you for clarifying. Do go on."

"OK. So, Dennis has been with the library since it began, not long after the Stedman became the home for that stupid book with the Twain notes in the margins that he found when he was in college. I was devoted to making my father tons of money and seeing him criticized in the media." The tears tumbled from her eyes. "Dennis told me in the church that now I am the beneficiary of the estate, I could put a stop to the Center." The younger woman looked beseechingly at Martha. "I was angry with him because that was the first thing he thought of after learning of Benjamin's death, but I was also angry that he'd assumed I'd want to kill Benjamin's dream. That's the kind of person I'd led him to believe I was."

Martha found herself crying along with Ana. "Sometimes it takes us longer than we wish—too long—to realize how selfish we've been," she said, going on to explain how she'd overlooked the signs that all was not well with Aunt Lorna until it was too late to turn back the clock. "All we can do is set ourselves on the best path forward and try as best we can to make the future different." For Martha, this meant keeping her aunt's beloved store open and caring for the dear friends Lorna had left behind. It meant pursuing the life her aunt had probably always wanted her to have: not just a job as a means of making a living, but one filled with happiness and purpose. She explained to Ana that she still wasn't sure she was totally comfortable with the new direction she'd set out on, but it felt right to her.

"I'm so sorry," she said finally. "Here I am going on and on about my own issues when you've just lost your father."

"But I'm glad you shared that. *I* need to think about *my* purpose, and what direction I want my life to go in," said Ana. "It's time for me to live *for* something, not *against* something."

While they had been talking, Ana had been sketching on a piece of copy paper.

"What are you drawing?" Martha asked.

"Oh, nothing really," Ana replied, turning the paper so Martha could see. It was a blue jay. Even in pencil, Ana had managed to capture the bird's defiant eye, sharp head crest, the telltale black necklace across its chest, and the white wing bar above its flank.

"Ana, that is amazing!" she cried.

Ana shrugged and gave a teary laugh. "Well, before I became an evil CFO, my first love was art. And I guess Benjamin's obsession with birds has rubbed off on me a bit. It always takes me back to my childhood in Brazil, and the exotic birds that perched in the trees outside my school. The blue jay was the first bird he taught me to identify in the U.S. He told me not to be fooled by their brilliant blue majesty, that they are actually quite aggressive and territorial, willing to do whatever necessary to keep what's theirs."

"Yikes!" Martha said. "And here I am feeding them outside the shop." She paused for a moment, then went on. "I wish I were more like you. I have a love of birds, but no financial brain to speak of."

"What do you mean? Is there something I could help with?"

Martha painted in broad terms the situation she was in with the shop and the house. "Things are in a holding pattern, but it's all pretty precarious."

"Do you have a business plan?" Ana asked.

"Well, some of the gals have been helping me." Martha detailed the work that the financially minded Margaret and local IT expert Joanne had been doing for her, as well as the idea to take Birds 'n' Beans custom roasts online.

"That's all a great start, and it sounds like you've done a fantastic job positioning yourself for online sales. But you'd really benefit, I think, from a written business plan. I'd be happy to go over what you need, if that would be helpful."

Excitement and doubt dueled in Martha's brain. Could she trust this young woman who'd undermined her own father's business? Given the shop's uneven financial footing, did she have a choice?

"Are you kidding?" asked Martha. "I'll take all the help you feel like giving, if it's not too much to ask at a time like this."

Ana smiled. "If you don't mind, I'd like to borrow your computer to begin writing Benjamin's—my father's—obituary. Once I've outlined that, I'd be happy to create a business plan for you. I'd be grateful for the distraction."

"Please, be my guest," Martha said, turning on and logging into the computer. "I'm going to go check on the rest of your friends." She shuddered as an unwelcome thought popped into her brain.

And see if one of them might just be a murderer.

Chapter Ten

Martha headed downstairs to the shop where PJ, Hannah, and one of the three campers were bustling about. The camper was the woman Scott Murphy had pointed at and accused of murder. At that moment, she was wiping down the empty tables.

Martha sidled up to her. "Is everything all right? Where are your friends?"

The woman gestured toward the front door and nodded. "Yes, everything is OK. My friends went back to the campground to rest. I figured I'd be better off helping out here, like PJ asked. Least I could do to thank you for the hospitality, and besides, I'm sick of being cooped up in my camper. My name is Shara Yang, by the way." She put her hand out and Martha shook it. Shara, who had a firm handshake—always a plus in Martha's book—was short and sported shiny straight black hair pushed back with a Buff headband.

"Nice to meet you, Shara. Did you three finish talking to Officer Daniels?"

"We did. There was really nothing much to say. We're all from Michigan. Retired faculty from a university up there. We've been up at the campground for the last week, hoping to take in some late birding before winter strands us all indoors until spring. I didn't even know about Marshall and his group being in this area until we arrived here earlier today, so I have no idea what Mr. Murphy was talking about and why he would accuse me of murder. But yes, I did know Mr. Marshall some years back. Haven't seen him since and wouldn't want a thing to do with him, then or now."

Martha caught the dislike in the petite woman's voice. "May I ask how you knew Mr. Marshall?"

"I used to be a professor of management. I met Marshall at a conference where he was the keynote speaker, got talking to him one day during the conference about working together. It never really panned out and it left a bad taste in my mouth, to be perfectly honest. But that was several years ago. I never really got to know him well, and it's nothing but a coincidence that I would be in the vicinity when he was killed." She shrugged, emphasizing her lack of emotion about the deceased man.

"What a strange coincidence, though," Martha said. "Anyway, thanks for helping out with things here. I think I'll go out and get some air, maybe check in on all of our visitors. I'm guessing they'll be hard at work by now."

"That was a brilliant move on your friend PJ's part, by the way. It's a classic emergency management technique I used to teach in my Organizational Development courses. Provide task-related focus in a crisis as a way of calming a group. Brilliant."

Martha laughed. "Yeah, PJ is smart in ways we mere mortals can only aspire to." She "suited up," as she'd come to refer to the process of donning close to every shred of winter gear she owned, then settled Penny with PJ and Hannah. The two seemed to be working themselves into another disagreement, so Martha made her getaway fast. She once again strapped on snowshoes and headed down the sidewalk. Passing Fins to Fur, she couldn't help glancing in and seeing snow drifting against the hiking sticks standing in a group near the shattered front door. She felt sick at the thought of what Jason had ahead of him.

Coming to the end of the walkway, she was about to take a left and head toward the library when a movement caught her eye. She looked up to the second floor of Toad in a Hole and saw Margaret and Octavius furiously flapping their arms to get her attention, motioning her to come around to the back where the apartment entrance was.

By the time Martha had snowshoed her way around the bookstore, Octavius was standing in his doorway. "Come in, Martha, come in! You'll catch your death out here," he said.

"Are you two OK?" Martha asked. "You looked rather frantic."

"Oh, we are perfectly marvelous!" he exclaimed. Martha looked a bit more closely and saw that his eyes were indeed more shiny and his cheeks ruddier than usual. "You must come in."

"OK, OK, but just for a few minutes. I need to go check on the hiking group. PJ has assigned them all jobs to do around the village, so I'm hoping to help Chip by picking up a bit more info on each of them to pass on to him. To help his investigative efforts, you understand."

Octavius laid a finger alongside his nose, added a knowing wink, and said, "Of course. You're just passing things on to Officer Daniels."

They started up the stairs and Octavius called out, "Margaret, take your brain out of XXX land. Martha is here."

"Oh, wonderful." As they entered the sitting room, Margaret closed her laptop and took off her kitty-cat glasses. She was still in the same chair she'd been in during Martha's last visit, and Martha took in an almost-empty tumbler of what she guessed was some kind of liqueur on the small side table next to her.

"Martha is doing some sleuthing," Octavius said with another exaggerated wink.

"I'm not really *sleuthing*," Martha said. "I'm helping Chip Daniels gather some information while simultaneously keeping our guests occupied."

"Ah-ha! *Oui, oui*! And what do you think of *zis*, Monsieur Poirot?" Margaret asked Octavius in a fake French accent.

"I think that Jane Tennison would be proud, very proud indeed," he replied in overly annunciated syllables.

"No, really," Martha protested, "I'm not trying to butt in where I don't belong—"

"My dear," said Octavius, drawing closer so Martha could smell the alcohol on his breath. *Sherry*, she thought. *Ugh*! "Please, by all means, *butt in*. Our Officer Daniels means well, but he is still in nappies compared to you. You have a way with people—a knack for drawing information out, even when they would not ordinarily share. I feel sure, and I'm guessing Margaret would agree, that you can figure out what happened to Mr. Marshall long before our young detective-in-training will hit puberty."

"Now, that's not quite fair and you both know it—"

"Enough, enough!" Octavius said, waving away Martha's protest. "We bade you come hither not to discuss murder, but to share our idea with you."

Margaret nodded, taking a not-very-ladylike last slurp from her glass.

"We've been thinking of what you said about the shopkeepers and how we need to keep a better watch on one another. You see, it's rather ironic, really. So many of us, myself included, came to Riley Creek to begin again. To reinvent. To create a new story for ourselves. Oh my! A new *story*? How apropos to my own entrepreneurial journey." He and Margaret guffawed to each other, and Martha felt like the designated driver at a geriatric bachelor party.

"But back to the point," Octavius continued, "we've been talking since you left about this. And we reflected that many of the shopkeepers came here in part to be left alone, to—as they say in the small but proud state of New Hampshire—live and let live. In a way, Riley Creek is so very good for that way of life, that in times like this, we realize how tenuous some of our connections to one another are. Perhaps it took a newcomer such as yourself to make us realize it."

Margaret picked up the narrative, her voice uncharacteristically clear and confident. "Octavius is right. Some of us who have lived here for a long time take so much pride in our self-sufficiency that we've lost sight of the ways in which we need to stay connected for lots of reasons, one of them being support in times of emergency. This emergency has made the two of us realize that we don't have a way of contacting or looking after everyone when we most need to. But we have an idea." Here, she looked at Octavius for support, peeking over the kitty-cat glasses that she seemed to have forgotten she'd already removed.

Octavius took up the dialogue. "My dear, we'd like to propose the creation of a shopkeepers' association. But that name doesn't quite suit, you see, because while some of us are shopkeepers, selling various items, others provide services, like yoga, beauty treatments, and the like. So we have an alternate nomenclature to suggest." Here he clasped his hands together at his chest, looking like a beauty queen waiting for the finalists to be announced. "We've come up with the R-C," he said proudly.

"The R-C? As in, Riley Creek?" Martha asked.

"The Retailers' Collective!" shouted Margaret.

"Wow," said Martha, trying to mirror their excitement, but at the moment, it was hard to think of much beyond the storm, the murder, and the need to reach the outside world.

"And we think you should be the group's first chairwoman!" said Octavius.

"What?" Martha was sure now that if these two were not three sheets to the wind, they were a definite two point five. "Why me? I only just got here!"

"That's exactly what makes you the perfect candidate," said Margaret. "Many of us villagers, like myself and Octavius here, are too set in our ways to look at this with new eyes. We need someone who can think outside the box, as you might say"—here, she snorted a fast laugh that was so out of place for Margaret, Martha wanted to look down at her shoes and pretend it didn't happen—"and realize what this group can do. Sure, it can be a kind of emergency telephone tree, but we've heard of other small towns that have associations that raise money, sponsor things, and make important decisions."

"Well, I don't think that's the worst idea in the world, but we'd need to talk to more of the merchants... er, retailers... to get their thoughts about a group like this. And I certainly think they'd want to vote on any leadership positions."

Martha thought back over her time on a college campus. Any decision required at least five committee meetings and a written proposal before it could be shot down and brought up again for reconsideration when a new leader was hired. That made her laugh inside. Standing here with these two inebriated seniors, she considered how far she'd traveled from that life.

And yet, it *was* a sound idea (the concept of the R-C, not the part about her being its leader). Martha and the other business owners could benefit from some kind of organization, she felt sure. But what should that look like?

"Margaret, Octavius, I agree that this is a great idea. And I think you should keep thinking on it. Perhaps without the sherry." Margaret blushed enough to let Martha know she wasn't completely plastered. "But for now, I need to go check in with our guests and get back in time to help PJ serve dinner at the shop. Would you care to join us?"

The two looked at each other in immediate agreement. "No," they said simultaneously. "We are quite comfortable here for the evening," added Octavius.

"Although, if I croaked in the storm, my first book would probably sell like hotcakes," hiccupped Margaret, realizing what she'd said and putting a hand over her mouth in embarrassment.

"We're reaching a critical *climax* in Chapter Five of Margaret's second book, so it's just as well we stay in."

All three were silent for a moment until Martha broke in. "Okey dokey, I think we're done here," she said, gearing up for her trip back outside. "If you change your mind, come on over when you see people beginning to gather."

Back out in the snow, Martha set a course for the Riley Creek Public Library. Because it was several blocks from the village green and the road leading there had not been well plowed, she had to work hard to snowshoe her way down the middle of the street, and was soon sweating under her clothes from the effort of pushing along the top of the heavy snow. It took about twenty minutes for her to reach the library.

Even covered in a few feet of snow, it was a marvel. Martha remembered when she was little and visiting Riley Creek with her parents, she could never understand how a small village could have such a grand library when her larger and more metropolitan hometown in northern Ohio had a library that fit into a modular building in the rear of the City County premises.

What she didn't know then, but did now thanks to Delores Ritzenwaller, was that the library had been the brainchild of Charlton Riley, often referred to as the "Father of Riley Creek." Martha couldn't bring up all the many details that Delores had relayed, but she did recall that the marble used in its construction came from Knoxville, Tennessee, and that same marble had been used in such famous buildings as the J.P. Morgan Library in New York, the U.S. Capitol and the National Gallery of Art in Washington, D.C. Martha had had no idea that as early as the 1850s, Knoxville had been well known for its marble quarrying and that the precious stone had been used in construction all across the U.S. up until the Great Depression.

Charlton Riley had recognized the importance of literacy to the small community and had raised money to fund the library's construction. *What a visionary he must have been!* Martha thought. While he could have dreamed up a one-room building well suited for the small village population back then, what he eventually brought to fruition was something much grander. As a child, Martha had called the library "the castle," and with good reason.

Two levels of broad marble steps led up to the enormous front doors, each one too heavy for Martha to budge back then, and only easier now thanks to the automatic opener button mounted to their right. To the right and left of the stairway were enormous marble pillars, and above the doors was elaborate scrollwork engraved into the stone. The "wings" of the library, which Martha knew now to be the spacious stacks inside, extended outward to the right and left. Altogether, the building was as imposing as it was beautiful, and now supported several communities, not just Riley Creek. All thanks to Charlton Riley's ability to see into the future.

Bet he was a reader, Martha reflected.

If Martha had been intimidated by the size of the structure as a child, that feeling was tempered by the knowledge of what lay beyond the heavy doors. Once they opened, the smell of literature flooded her nose, and a whole world of book-borrowing possibilities became hers. Aunt Lorna would bring her here as often as she'd asked as a child, and on each visit, Martha would borrow a tote bag full of books. She remembered seeing doubt on the librarian's face when she'd checked out so many books, but she'd merely accepted this as an unspoken challenge.

Martha had loved books then and she loved them now, but her passion had deepened and developed maturity. She could no longer read a bag of books in a week or two, but her love of libraries and their untapped secrets still gave her an uncomplicated feeling of possibility. What mystery existed in the world that could not be solved in the stacks of the library?

Martha pushed on the automatic door opener from habit, simultaneously realizing that it would not work without electricity. Putting her whole body into it, she pulled the three-inch-thick door open. As her eyes adjusted to the dim natural light inside, she registered a few things that had changed since she'd come here as a kid in her bathing suit and flip-flops. The massive wooden card catalog that used to stand to the right of the entrance was now part of an historical display in the corner entitled "Libraries of Yesteryear." Now when she approached the desk to check out a book, the library staff used a handheld scanner to "beep" it instead of asking her to fill out a lending card tucked in an envelope in the back of the book. And there was always the fact that, if it weren't for the electricity being out, she could just stay home and borrow most books online, in the form of an eBook or audiobook.

I like the real thing, though, she thought, wondering momentarily if she'd have any time to sneak away and read on her camp mattress that evening. Though she loved her current Shugak mystery, she had other books piled next to her bed back at her cottage equally deserving of her attention. *I turned fifty-two last month, which means half of my reading life is behind me. I can't afford to waste any precious time.*

No one was at the desk to greet her, so she took the liberty of removing and hanging her layers with those already on the coat rack to the left of the front door.

"Yoo-hoo!" came Delores's voice as the elderly woman herself floated across the main floor, a sleek-looking headlamp strapped on her head and casting a surprisingly bright glow. As she approached Martha, she reached up to angle the light down so that it didn't shine in Marth's eyes. "I didn't expect to see you, but I'm glad you're here," she said, placing two volumes on the library counter. "I found something you need to see."

Chapter Eleven

"What is it?" Martha asked without preamble. She picked up the two books. The first, titled *Sir E*, claimed to be a "very unabridged biography" of Sir Elton John. Martha looked down at the second book. It promised its readers it was a "very, *very* unauthorized biography" of Bette Midler. The author's name on both volumes was Scott Murphy.

"There's more," said Delores, stepping behind the circulation desk. She flipped through a few magazines, selecting the one she'd been looking for. It was from the previous year and appeared to be a small review of Murphy's Midler biography. Martha skimmed it, the words making her wince.

Scott Murphy is back with what must be the year's worst book. He claims that it's a very, very unauthorized biography of Bette Midler, one of America's favorite performers on stage and screen. Why, then, would Murphy not go to the trouble that other biographers have gone to and publish an authorized biography so that we can get the facts right?

Because he, like so many others, is downright lazy. Murphy twists facts to suit his narrative, and readers should be careful before believing a single gossipy word that comes out of this author's keyboard. Like Kitty Kelley before him, Murphy has a loose relationship with the truth, and we predict an even looser relationship with book sales. Abandon hope, all ye who think about reading this.

"Ouch," said Martha. Was there another word stronger than scathing? *Roasting? Eviscerating?* Those might be more accurate. "What does the reviewer mean, 'Like Kitty Kelley before him'?" she asked Delores. The name sounded like someone out of an Old West television show.

"Oh, Kitty Kelley is well known in the literary world," said Delores. "Well, on second thought, perhaps 'literature' isn't the right word to use to describe her work."

Martha tried to be patient, but her strategy of staying silent to encourage others to speak was becoming more and more frustrating. Luckily, Delores got to the point.

"Kitty Kelley is probably the most well-known American writer of unauthorized biographies. She's written about Oprah, Nancy Reagan and several others. But her most famous unauthorized biography was about Frank Sinatra. He actually sued her to keep her from publishing, but he dropped the lawsuit as I recall. She went on to publish it and sold tons of copies. Made the bestseller list back then, I believe."

"I don't really know that much about unauthorized biographies. Why do people get so upset about them? I might be flattered if someone wanted to write a book about me."

Delores nodded. "Well, that's one way to look at it. But think about this: what if someone writes a book about you and includes things that are not true, or that you have no way to offer your perspective on? And you know the public. The more salacious, the better. They may read an unauthorized biography about you and assume it's all true and that the author checked their facts."

"Yes, you've got a point. I never thought about it like that. I guess in that case, it could be sort of an unpopular genre."

"But it certainly sells. Every time a new one comes out, we have wait lists for people to check out both the hard copies in the library and the eBook and audiobook versions."

"So if Murphy is an unauthorized biography writer, why was he along with Benjamin Marshall on this trip? It looks like Marshall's biography was going to be authorized—that seems odd, doesn't it?"

"That's what I thought. And the great detectives always keep an eye out for inconsistencies," Delores said with a wink. "Which is why I wanted to bring it to your attention."

"The plot does thicken," agreed Martha.

Delores led Martha downstairs to check on the Allens. When they'd arrived, Delores explained, she had trained Fred on a volunteer task that was desperately in need of doing. This close to the holidays, it was hard to attract enough volunteers to keep up with the library's many services. Martha followed Delores to the basement level where piles and piles of books waited on wooden carts to be placed in their proper positions on the correct shelves. Here she found Fred Allen, alphabetizing the top shelf of one of the carts.

"Even though the library is officially closed due to the weather, you never know if a child might stop by. If one does, someone ought to be at the circulation desk to greet them." With that, Delores turned and headed back up the stairs. Martha watched her with a swelling heart before turning to Fred.

"Hi, Fred, how goes it?" she asked. "I'm just checking on each of our guests to see how they are doing. Thank you so much for helping Delores."

"You kidding? It's the least we could do for the hospitality you've all shown us," he said. Now that Martha was closer and in a more relaxed setting, she took in some details about the man she'd neglected to observe before. Of medium height with soft brown eyes and close-cropped black hair flecked with grey, he was not unattractive for his age. She guessed from what he'd told her about his time at Harvard Business School in the late '70s that he might have been in his early sixties or seventies. His small rimless glasses looked feather-light.

Bet those cost a pretty penny, she thought, her eyes widening as they were pulled down to the giant silver timepiece on his wrist.

"Is that a TAG Heuer watch?" she asked.

Clearly embarrassed, Fred answered her sheepishly. "Yes, it is. Frieda gives me a hard time about it. Their slogan—or at least, it used to be—is 'Don't crack under pressure.' She got it for me years ago as a way to remember not to lose myself too much in my work. Not sure it worked, but I sure love this watch."

"How's it going with the books?" Martha asked.

"Going fine, actually. We each took several carts of books to put away. I'm still working on alphabetizing mine, while ea-gle-eye Frieda could spot the shelving numbers for hers from miles away. So she's already finished hers and is on to her next assignment." He chuckled. "Do you know this is the first time I've stepped foot in a public library in over twenty years?"

Martha smiled in response. Going for breezy rather than nosey, she asked, "Didn't you say you have children? Seems like you'd have gone in one if you had any munchkins."

"Oh, we have two amazing boys. Well, men, actually. All grown up and doing well for themselves. And yes, they frequented the library when they were young, but mostly with their mom. For better or for worse, my work exploded during their early years, and I was traveling from office to office, overseeing product development, mergers, all kinds of things. Frieda traveled with me when the kids could stay with her parents or mine. We went all over the world and had some amazing adventures back then. Yep, those were some crazy years." He shook his head from side to side.

"And now?" Martha asked. "It sounds like you do some kind of private investing."

"The idea was that when I retired from the telecom business, I'd have more time to spend at home. But by that time, the boys were more self-sufficient and venture capitalism had taken off. Things were hot and if we were going to move, we had to move fast, especially as the dot com businesses started to pop up everywhere." He held his hands up and made popping gestures in the air, like fireworks exploding on the fourth of July.

"I was lucky and had lots of successes, which have positioned us well as a family and make me eligible to invest even more substantial sums now. I like to think that I'm carrying on a tradition started by my grandfather. He was a sharecropper who finally saved enough to buy his own small piece of land. Benjamin's Center was the next project I was investigating. It looked amazingly promising." He shook his head forlornly. "I still can't believe what's happened. I mean, who would want to hurt Benjamin?"

Who indeed?

"I don't know, Fred," Martha said, "but I do know once this storm passes, we'll get to the bottom of it."

Martha left Fred wheeling his cart into the stacks as she went in search of Frieda. After Frieda's success with the re-shelving, Delores had set her to work on filling book requests for the library's homebound patrons, another activity that was severely backed up due to volunteer shortage. Taking the twists and turns that Delores had described to her, Martha followed the sounds of rustling plastic and found Frieda surrounded by piles and piles of books stacked on four large tables.

"Oh my gosh!" Martha said. "You look like you're in danger of literally becoming buried in books."

"I know." Frieda's voice sounded even deeper than normal in the cavernous basement space. "It's hard to imagine that they usually have several people down here, toiling away on these homebound orders. Kind of gives me the creeps!" She demonstrated a whole-body shiver for emphasis.

Like her husband, Frieda looked like she'd walked out of the pages of an Orvis catalog, but with some unique touches that gave her a distinctive style. Though she'd tied a long red scarf around her head, the odd curl of hair had slipped out of place. She wore simple silver hoops about two inches in diameter, and matching silver bangles that clinked together musically as she worked.

How is it that some women can be accidentally fashionable, while I can't pull it off even when I try? Martha thought.

"I just came from visiting Fred and he's working really hard on the book shelving. We are all so grateful for your willingness to help out our little village while we wait to make contact with the 'outside world.'" Martha provided air quotes to these last two words, paying homage to Frieda's probable dismay at being stuck here in Riley Creek and downplaying the sense that they were truly unattached to the world beyond. In cold truth Martha knew that, until the storm let up some, for all intents and purposes they were totally cut off.

Frieda took her hands out of the bag she was working on, brushed her forehead with the back of a bangled wrist, and said, "Nonsense. We're happy for the distraction, and happy to give back in some small way. To be honest, I wasn't sure what I was going to do with myself if we had to sit around much longer. You're doing us a favor by giving us work to do." She moved the bag away to join what Martha guessed was a pile of others containing finished orders.

"Fred told me that you used to take your boys to the library quite often. They are grown up now, I understand."

"Surprised he remembers that," Frieda said. "It was important to me that the boys realize the value of education. They've always enjoyed reading, though truth be told, these days they're more taken with their careers."

"Like father, like sons, I guess, if they enjoy reading. Fred must have done his share of that if he attended the Harvard Business School."

Frieda gave a wry laugh. "Ha! He and his friends spent more time trying to count their pennies in their investment club meetings than studying in the library. It was me who was hanging out in the library more often than not. While I was at Radcliffe."

"Radcliffe? Wow! What did you—" Martha stopped herself before she could voice the age-old and somewhat vacuous question: *what did you do for work?* Now that she was no longer a card-carrying member of the rat race, she realized just how often she was tempted to introduce herself, or ask others to introduce themselves through their professional identities. She'd almost just done the same thing with Frieda Allen.

"Oh, it's OK," said Frieda. "I know what you were going to ask and I get that all the time. A woman with a Radcliffe education must have had a career, right? Well, that was the plan, but as the saying goes, plans change. I'd originally planned to graduate from Radcliffe and attend the Harvard Business School to get my MBA, but... I met Fred while he was at Harvard and I was at Radcliffe and we fell in love. His career took off, two kids happened, and thirty plus years later, here I am."

Martha smiled. "But what a wonderful life you must have. From what Fred said, your boys are doing great and he has had a successful professional life, and you and he got to travel a whole bunch. That feels light years more productive than what my life is at the moment."

Frieda asked her a bit about the shop and Martha gave her an abridged version, leaving out the previous fall's murders as well as the shop's bleak financial position.

"I admire you more than you know, trying to make it as an independent businesswoman. That's very similar to where I saw my life going before it took a right turn. Don't get me wrong; I wouldn't trade the boys for anything. They attended Groton Academy and have a secure financial future, I'm on two women's pickleball teams and I work out at a private gym five mornings a week. I even have fairly influential roles on a couple of foundations that sponsor awards in the millions of dollars, so I feel I make a difference. But that's... different from making your own mark as you're doing here in Riley Creek."

"It's a team effort, for sure," Martha said, explaining how the gals had taken her under their wing so she could establish herself in the village, and were helping her now to create an on-line retail presence in order to boost sales.

"You are fortunate as well, just in a different way," said Frieda. "But, Martha, be careful... it sounds like your aunt's friends want nothing other than the best for you, but keep your own counsel. I've known far too many women who were taken advantage of by those they trusted, only to be betrayed by them later."

The look on Martha's face must have shown her confusion.

"Oh listen to me, carrying on and giving you advice," Frieda said. "I'm a country-club mother and wife with nothing but First World problems to occupy her time."

Sensing it was the moment to change the subject, Martha said, "You both must be devastated by the loss of Mr. Marshall. I'm so sorry."

Frieda nodded. "You know, having lived with my husband and sons after growing up with two older brothers, I've come to realize that men form friendships very differently than women. For one thing, they have fewer of them, and fewer still are meaningful. Sure, they have lots of acquaintances, but not so much what you and I might consider real friends.

"Fred was one of only a few African Americans in his MBA cohort the year he graduated, so having a real friend like Benjamin meant the world to him back then, whether he knew it or not. Even though Benjamin was a bit older, they clicked from the start. And then, he was there for Benjamin when Benjamin stumbled, first with Ana's mother and later with some other high-profile messes he found himself in. And there have been some doozies. No matter what happened, Fred was always there for Benjamin to turn to and get advice.

"In some ways, I think Fred was disappointed that *he* was never the one to lead the high-flying, jet-setting life that Benjamin had. But at the same time, when the chips were down, he was also relieved to never have been in the spotlight like Benjamin often was. The boys and I could never get enough of Fred's time, but when Benjamin needed him, he somehow found the time to be available to help."

Martha thought she detected a hint of resentment, even though Frieda's voice remained light.

"But Fred sounds very successful and busy now," Martha said. "Did it all even out somehow, do you think? Fred got the success, but without the drama?"

"Yes, something like that," said Frieda, giving Martha a smile that did not quite reach her eyes.

"Do you mind if I ask you one more thing?" Martha said.

"Of course. What is it?" Frieda reached for a new bag, pulling out the book order inside and searching for the first title in the piles that lay around her.

"Do you know much about Mr. Murphy? I'm trying to help Officer Daniels with some background so he doesn't need to gather it later. He interviewed Mr. Murphy back at the shop, but it was brief, so I was wondering if there was anything you might have known since you all had been hiking together."

"Well, one thing I can tell you is that man was not made for hiking or roughing it. You may be surprised to hear that I was raised on a farm, and I know how to make it in the wilderness. That guy is what you'd call a 'city slicker' through and through.

He brought brand new boots to hike in—rookie mistake—and could barely unroll his sleeping bag.

"As to how he knew Benjamin, this sounds crazy, but Fred told me he'd been a bartender at an event for the Stedman and that was where Benjamin met him. Next thing Fred knew, Scott was invited to be Benjamin's biographer and then, later, to go on this little jaunt with us to get to know Benjamin better. Other than that, I don't know too much about him except that he hung on everything Benjamin said, as if Benjamin was the Second Coming. Like Scott was desperate, somehow. I'm not sure what happens now, since the subject of his book is dead."

Martha was a bit taken aback by the coarseness of Frieda's words, but she chalked it up to the long day and difficult circumstances they were all doing their best to cope with.

"I don't really know either. It's just awful all around." Pausing a few beats, she then added, "Well, thanks. I really have enjoyed talking to you. See you at the shop later tonight for dinner?"

Frieda confirmed that she and Fred would be there.

Speaking of dinner, Martha thought as she climbed the stairs and headed out of the library, *you two certainly have given me something to chew on. For starters, why do you both seem so calm in the face of your so-called "good friend" Benjamin Marshall's death?*

Chapter Twelve

Martha snowshoed back to the village center and thought the storm felt just a fraction lighter than before. Shadows had lengthened across the brick storefronts, the early darkness of winter moving in. Emerging around the corner and onto the green, she spotted Jason standing outside of Fins to Fur, hands on hips, gazing up at the gigantic tree that lay smack dab across his business.

"Not sure you'll get it to move through force of will alone," she said to him, trying for equal parts levity and sympathy.

"Man, do I wish I could. Who knows how long it'll take to get someone up here to remove it, even after the roads open back up. I was thinking of going to my dad's place to get my insurance policy, so I'd at least know what coverage I've got." He looked at her doubtfully. "You wouldn't want to come along, would you?"

"Sure, why not?" she said. "PJ is watching Penny, and I swear that dog has slept through most of this blizzard. But where's Scott?"

"Well, we did our assignment. We shoveled off all of the sidewalks on the green, and shoveled out all of those cars"—here, he gestured at the handful of vehicles parked around the square that earlier had just been white lumps—"and by that time, I've gotta admit, even I was winded. And Mr. City Slicker was dead tired. He just wanted to get back to his precious computer. I gave the guy a break and told him he could finish and go back to Birds 'n' Beans, as long as he stayed out of everyone's way. Tell PJ I'm sorry, will ya?"

"Oh, I have a feeling PJ can handle Scott," said Martha.

"Let me pop into the shop for a few supplies, and then we'll head over to Dad's," Jason said, heading for the front door of Fins to Fur.

"Whoa, are you nuts?" Martha said, grabbing Jason's arm and pulling him back. "It's not safe to go in there with that tree on the place."

"It's fine. I've been in a few times and the tree is firmly resting on the roof and attic supports. I'll just be a minute." He turned back to the store, then faced her again. "I didn't know you cared." Martha rolled her eyes as Jason stepped into the dark store.

Ten minutes later, they piled into Jason's four-wheel drive and made their way ploddingly to his childhood home. Thankfully, much of the route to Jason's father's house was overhung by the boughs of giant pines, so they enjoyed patches of clear road. The biggest challenge was visibility as the misting snow continued to blow straight into the low beams of Jason's headlights.

The house sat back a good distance from the main road and the driveway was one massive snowdrift. Jason reached behind his seat and pulled two sets of snowshoes into his lap. He handed one to Martha, and then they each opened their door and strapped the shoes on before jumping into the snow. Jason shouldered a small pack and they started the trek to the front door.

Martha marveled at the silence, the glint of the snow reflecting like glass. Her mind drifted off to *shinrin yoku*, Japanese for "forest bathing," and she wondered if the same health benefits that came from it applied to this frozen landscape.

They reached the front door in a few minutes and Jason unlocked it, using strong pushes to get it open as it had frozen to its frame. And then they were in. It took a moment for Martha's brain to adjust to the utter silence of the house after the howling wind that had been her perpetual white noise these last few days. Jason set his pack down and pulled out a small battery-powered lantern. It cast an impressive amount of light around the den.

Den, Martha thought. *Even the word makes me feel like a kid again.* Though the air in the house was stale, there was something about its scent that pulled Martha back to her childhood. She and Jason and a few other Riley Creek kids had spent time in this house in the years before his dad's drinking had become so bad that he didn't invite them over anymore.

Martha couldn't remember the last time she'd seen actual wallpaper on a wall, but here, it was all around the dining area: cream base decorated with olive green velveteen paisleys she used to reach out and stroke when she was little. Taking her snowy boots off and placing them on the rug by the door, she sunk her wool-socked feet into the shag carpeting (rusty orange, if memory served her right, but it was too dark to tell).

The wood-paneled living room area was also just as she remembered it. The television was gargantuan, a behemoth alongside today's slender flat screens. Sitting on a chunky plastic end table next to a leather recliner (*probably an actual La-Z-Boy*, Martha thought) was a television remote control the size of a telephone base circa 1975. A hand-knit afghan fell over the back of the matching worn leather couch, above which hung several framed studio pictures of Jason, showing his progression from infant to young man.

As much as the space felt familiar to Martha, it held an eerie tinge. It was like *The Land That Time Forgot*, even though she doubted Jason had forgotten much. She heard Jason moving through the house, up and down the stairs, in and out of doors, squeaking open the faucets.

"No broken pipes so far and I found my insurance policy. I'll read it when we get back to town," he said, rejoining her downstairs and knocking on the crown of his head for luck as they'd all done when they were kids. "Care to join me in the other room?"

She followed him through the kitchen, another shrine to the '70s and '80s. As they pushed through the galley door and into the room beyond, Martha was surprised to see a small fire burning in the hearth. Looking around quickly, she recognized the "formal living room," which in most homes was seldom used. This one was very well preserved, with plastic covering the two couches that sat parallel to one another along either wall.

Two beanbag chairs had been positioned alongside the fire, and Jason plopped into one. From his pocket he extracted a metal flask and unscrewed it, holding it up to her.

"May I interest you in a pre-dinner cocktail?" he asked.

"Well, without the fire it would have been a definite no, but since you asked so nicely..." She reached out and accepted the flask, taking a small sip. Whatever it was burned all the way down, but the warmth kept her from complaining.

"Fireball," he said. "I barely drink at all anymore, except for utilitarian purposes, and I'm going to say this definitely qualifies." He took a long swig and blew out. "Whew. That really *does* burn."

Martha eased herself down into the other beanbag and put her hands and feet out in the direction of the fire. Now that it was growing a bit in intensity, Jason added a good-sized log.

"What a couple of days," he said, wiping his face with both hands. "I'm not crazy about this place, but I gotta admit it's nice to be away from town for a little while."

Nodding in agreement, Martha said, "It sure is. Still, your mom would kill us if she knew we were having a drink in her formal living room. Did you say you lived here with your dad when you first came back?"

"Yep. *That* was an amazing several months. It only worked because most of the time I was working on the shop with some contractor guys I'd met over in Park Ridge. We had to gut the whole thing so I more or less lived there for the first year. But even in the time I was here at the house with Dad, I saw enough to know he couldn't stay here. He was in bad shape."

"From his drinking?" Martha asked sympathetically. Jason's dad had escalated from what Aunt Lorna had euphemistically called a "social drinker" decades ago, and Martha wondered what Jason had come home to after so many years.

"The drinking, cirrhosis, his age, my mom's death... you name it. He'd been here by himself since he'd lost the car lot, and it was a mess. He had his groceries delivered by Piggly Wiggly, but he'd basically stopped washing dishes or cleaning the house. It was awful. I did as much as I could while getting the shop ready, and Mr. Jeremiah helped me get named as Dad's conservator so I could take care of the bills, his meds, and everything else. I moved him to the nursing center in Park Ridge almost a year ago now. You can guess how *that* went over with him."

Martha could only imagine what Jason had gone through, returning to his hometown and all of the difficult memories it held, only to face an even more challenging scenario with his elderly alcoholic dad.

"The worst moment was actually move-in day. The center director found all of the bottles he'd tried to smuggle in. Poured every last one out, right in front of Dad. She told him he was already dying, but that she was not going to allow him to hurry it along while he lived in *her* center. I'll let you guess the choice words he let out. But by then, he was too weak to do much more than bluster. It was sad, really. I go out to visit him every weekend I can, but we never had much to talk about and there's even less now. He's lost so much weight and is in a wheelchair. But actually, I think he's mellowed some. It's like he doesn't have anyone or anything to be mad at over there, so he's just waiting. For whatever comes next. But we can afford the care, thanks to his savings, and they are nice people."

Martha had just listened so far, but sensed he'd come to the end of his story.

"Jason, you're a good son to make sure you found a place where he'd be well cared for. It's more than some kids do."

Jason nodded, then ran his eyes over the room. "But what to do with this place? Dad made me promise not to sell it, in case he got well enough to come home."

"Well, I guess hold on to it until you're sure the time is right. I suspect you'll know what to do then."

"And what about you?" asked Jason. "You decided to come home to ol' Riley Creek too, make a go of it as a business owner. That seems really unlike you."

"What do you mean?" she asked, trying not to be offended, but hearing a hint of sharpness in her question. "You're not the only person who can run a successful business, you know."

Jason held his hands up in surrender. "No, no. It's just—it's like I said to you a few weeks back. You always seemed to want bigger, more, different, farther away when we were kids. The world owed you an adventure and by God, you were going to go out and get it." He took another swig from the flask.

"Things changed a bit when my folks died, of course, and in a way I had my adventure. I moved to a big city, had a career, and was doing pretty well, I suppose."

"That sounds... very adult," Jason said, barely hiding a smirk.

"You know, just because I didn't go out west to find my fame and fortune doesn't make me a total loser." She felt her anger flare and Jason put both hands up again.

"I'm sorry, I'm sorry!" he said. "I didn't mean it as a put-down. It's just... it sounds like you did well for yourself, but if you don't mind me saying, when you talk about Boston, you don't seem like you were very happy."

Martha's anger died down. He was right. She couldn't deny it.

"I thought that moving to a big city, finishing school and becoming self-sufficient was the adventure I wanted. And in some ways, it was. I accomplished a lot. But what I'm doing now, trying to run Birds 'n' Beans and keep everything afloat, feels a lot riskier than anything I did in my twenties and thirties. Oh, and in my forties." *Good gravy, am I really in my fifties?* she reflected, not for the first time. "But, to be honest, and it may sound crazy, I'm a lot happier than I've been in a long time."

She stopped, suddenly aware that she was revealing way more than she'd intended, and turned the questions on Jason.

"What about you? I know you mentioned back in the fall that you'd gone west and things hadn't gone as well as you'd hoped. Tell me more about that."

Jason laughed. "Well, for a while it was fantastic. I got accepted into the U of Colorado in Boulder, and I loved it. Made good friends, got into rafting, rock climbing and every other outdoor thing you can think of. My dad had been sure I'd wash out first semester, but I did better academically than even I had expected. So Dad being Dad, he decided not to give me any more money for college unless I switched my major from outdoor education to business so I could help him at the car lot after I graduated. I told him no way, and added some choice words about his profession, and that was that. Cut off, no money, and living halfway across the country. There was no way I was going to let my dad win, so I managed to leave school with my associate's degree and I hit the road to the Rockies."

Martha prompted him to go on. "But wasn't that good in a way? Isn't that what you loved? Being in nature?"

"At that time, I thought so. I was a rafting guide during the week and went rock climbing all weekend. I started taking pills to stay awake Monday to Friday, and then other pills to get some sleep on the weekends." He scratched both sides of his ginger beard, then looked down in embarrassment. "Let's just say somewhere along the line, taking pills morphed into selling pills, and eventually I got arrested. Did time with some of the most lowlife individuals you can imagine. Saw things in prison that..." He trailed off, evidently not wanting to elaborate.

"Anyway, shortly after I was released, Mom passed away and left me some money. I put it in the bank and never spent a cent. One day, I looked around at my minimum-wage life and decided it was time to come home. Maybe in part to see if I still had a home here." He looked around at the house, as if taking stock.

"I found an old man I once hated who now needed me and I could see things from his side a little bit more. When I think about it now, all the words that we both said way back when I was a kid, it makes me almost physically sick. I rejected him, his livelihood, and everything this place stood for. True, he was an alcoholic asshole, but I wonder how much I might have contributed to his issues by being such a difficult kid." Jason fell quiet.

"Jason, your dad's alcoholism was not your fault. No way," Martha objected.

"I guess all I'm saying is I wish I wouldn't have said some of the things I said. But we can't turn back the clock, can we?" Jason was quiet for a beat, then said, "Adulting stinks sometimes."

"And I bet your dad feels exactly the same about turning back the clock," Martha said. "But the important thing is now, and you are doing the very best you can by him. When it counts. You know, Aunt Lorna taught me one thing—well, she taught me one thing that's really gotten me through some tough times. She said that no matter what happens, you've got to keep on keepin' on, and I think that's exactly what you've done to take care of things for your dad."

"Thanks, Martha. I really mean it. Thanks. And thanks to my mom leaving me a small nest egg, I'm trying to do things better this time around." He sat up in his beanbag and flashed his John Wayne smile. "It's a fresh start for me. What do you say we try a fresh start too?"

Martha felt a ripple in her stomach that she hadn't experienced in a long time. Squirming a bit against the beans in her beanbag, she replied, "Jason, I'm really glad for you—for both of us—that we're trying for a fresh start to our lives. But you know Teddy and I—"

Jason cut her off. "Oh, so it's *Teddy* now, is it? Not even Chief Perry?" He smiled again, taunting her just like old times.

"Very funny. Yes, Chief Perry—Teddy—and I have been spending a lot of time together lately. I'd like to see where that goes."

Jason sat up straight, his eyes wide. "Oh. Wait a minute, Martha, I'm sorry, but I think you misunderstood. I wasn't asking you out. I literally was saying that I hoped we could make a fresh start of our friendship."

Martha felt her face burn with humiliation. "Oh yeah. Totally. Yeah, I knew that was what you meant. I was just... sharing, that's all. Ya' know, like friends do."

"Sure, I get it," Jason responded, looking as embarrassed as Martha felt. "Umm, do you think maybe we'd better get back? I've got these insurance papers to read and it's getting pretty dark out."

"Yes, right, it's time to get back. Definitely," said Martha.

Jason brought in a bucket of snow and doused the fire while Martha felt a flicker of something—what had that been?—go dark deep within her.

Chapter Thirteen

Jason drove back into the village. Though she couldn't prove it, Martha sensed that he drove with a bit more urgency than he had on the way out to his father's house. She sat pressed against the cold truck door, trying to stop replaying in her mind the embarrassing exchange they'd had.

Rounding the corner into the square, they noticed right away another bonfire was burning. Only a few buildings fronting the square had any light coming from their windows, so the bonfire and the illumination from Birds 'n' Beans stood out like beacons.

"Wonder what the occasion is this time?" Martha said, pointing to the bonfire. She could make out several people in the shop.

"Maybe it's to celebrate dinnertime," Jason replied. "I sure hope so. All that shoveling earlier made me hungry."

He parked the truck and they moved toward Birds 'n' Beans. Then Jason stopped. Martha turned to him.

"What is it?" she asked, guarding for bad news.

"Do you feel that?" Jason said, looking around.

"Feel what?"

"The snow. It's stopped."

Indeed it had. For the first time in two days, Martha could not feel the sting of snow on her cheeks as she moved from the vehicle to the building. She'd been scrunched down in her jacket so deeply and so intent on getting away from Jason that she'd not even noticed.

"So it has," she said. "So it has." *Please let this be a good sign,* she thought.

They opened the door to the shop and entered a pine-scented winter wonderland. Tea candles had been placed in jars on each of the tables, and music from *The Nutcracker* came through a speaker on the once-upon-a-time soda shop counter. Next to the speaker stood various bottles of wine and spirits, several already open, a bucket of ice and plastic cups. Pinecones were scattered haphazardly around the makeshift bar. Penny was in her dog bed, methodically gnawing away at something rawhide. Martha rarely let her eat such doggie delicacies for fear she'd gain too much weight, but decided she deserved a night of celebration just as much as her humans did.

A pine tree that was as wide as it was tall had been placed in the corner of the shop. It leaned a bit haphazardly against the wall, but its girth more than supported it. Twinkling white lights had been strung around it as well as chains of paper snowflakes. Magnolia boughs decorated almost every surface in the shop, even the top of the Royal roaster. Martha detected the smell of fresh bread and something even more savory. And, of course, coffee. She couldn't determine what kind with so many other scents competing, but she suddenly realized that she, like Jason, was ravenous.

Ellie, Pat, Jimmy, Delores and the Allens sat together around one table, sipping from plastic cups and talking amiably. Ellie and Frieda had their chairs turned slightly toward each other and seemed to be deeply involved in conversation. Carl, Cat, Lew, Helen, Don and two of the female campers were gathered at another table and looked to be in the throes of a very serious game of UNO. As Martha was watching, Lew hurled a card onto the pile with dramatic flair, threw up his arms and cried, "YES!"

An all-around groan came from the rest of the players, with Helen holding up her single remaining card and exclaiming, "No fair! I was *this close*!"

Scott Murphy was sitting near the front window with a mug in his hand, watching the room. He appeared to be contented for the first time since Martha had met him. His laptop, for once, was in its case and hanging with his jacket on the back of his chair.

The festive atmosphere was such a relief to Martha. The last two days had been full of tension, first with the storm, then the call to come to the church to help with the stranded hikers, the discovery of Marshall's body, the lack of contact with the outside world. This scene felt normal, but at the same time, Martha wondered if it was the right thing to do so soon after the death of one of the hikers.

She left Jason at the makeshift wine bar and went to talk to PJ, whom she could see along with Shara and Hannah through the pass-through window to the kitchen. Walking up to the window, she gestured PJ over. PJ threw a kitchen towel over her broad shoulder and leaned toward Martha.

"Well, what do you think?" she asked with a big grin. For the first time, Martha noticed the glitter-covered Christmas bulb earrings dangling from PJ's lobes.

"It's lovely, PJ, but where's Ana? What will she say when she—"

At that moment, Ana Moreno stepped down from the stairway and into the shop. Her tousled hair and puffy eyes advertised that she'd recently slept, and Martha watched as she took in the transformed setting. The room grew noticeably quieter. Martha saw that she wasn't the only one wondering how Marshall's daughter would feel about the festive atmosphere so soon after her father's murder.

Martha immediately went to her side. "Ana, are you OK? I went to the library and ended up visiting with the Allens and Delores for quite some time, then went to Jason's parents' house with him—" She stopped when she heard herself babbling.

PJ approached. "Honey," he said to Ana, placing a comforting arm around the young woman's shoulders, "I hope you don't find my little idea in bad taste, but I felt like your father's friends, and my friends, needed a little TLC tonight. And you probably do too. It's been a long few days, the holidays are just around the corner, and... well, I thought a special evening might go a long way for folks." PJ glanced over to the kitchen from where Hannah and Shara watched, their eyes full of guarded anticipation. From the look of the shop, the three had worked hard since breakfast.

From the hallway of Silent Sisters came a booming, "My God, this place looks like Christmas threw up all over it!" Ethel Jean came striding in, Tanner trailing behind. While Ethel Jean looked invigorated and ready to tangle, Tanner looked exhausted. She pointed a thumb back over her shoulder at her silver-haired assistant, who was adjusting his tortoiseshell glasses so that they sat straighter on his nose. "Who'd have known this guy was so strong?" she said, laughing and shaking her head.

"He carried extra inventory over from my duplex for almost two hours, then spent the last hour working on displays."

Tanner plopped down in a seat with a glass of wine, took a long drink, then closed his eyes. PJ and Martha turned back to Ana. The room had yet to recover the buzz it had enjoyed before her arrival, and Martha sensed many not wanting to return to full enjoyment until they gauged the young woman's reaction.

Martha reached out to touch Ana's arm. "Ana, are you—"

"I'm fine," Ana said, letting out an exhale. "I worked on your marketing plan and think I've got a decent draft for you. Then I fell asleep on one of the cots. Can you imagine? I guess I was just exhausted from everything." She trailed off and was quiet for a few moments.

Before either PJ or Martha could say more, Ana continued. "And, PJ, I think this is just perfect. You're right. It's been a terrible couple of days, and as bizarre as this sounds, this is exactly what my father would love. If he were here, he'd probably shout, 'Celebrating before the End of Days!' or something equally irreverent. I can't think of a better way for all of us to blow off steam and celebrate his spirit a little bit."

PJ and Martha both smiled, and all around the room and in the kitchen, shoulders relaxed.

Mary Jane and Frank walked in with Margaret and Octavius in tow. The pair from the bookshop seemed a little steadier on their feet than earlier, so Martha assumed that they must have slowed down on the sherry after she left. They had also clearly changed their minds about joining everyone else for dinner.

"The bad news is that Chip insisted on staying at the police station. The good news is that it stopped snowing!" Frank yelled to the room. A collective round of applause rose up.

"I shall take that as a signal to commence the festivities!" PJ cried, and waved to Hannah and Shara. "Clear the tables!" she yelled, and the UNO cards disappeared.

Hannah and Shara began shuttling plates to tables as the four newcomers joined Scott, as did Ana. Martha caught Scott giving Shara a long look before he was pulled into his table's conversation. Onto each table was placed a crusty loaf of bread with a serrated knife. Everyone looked to Carl to acknowledge his baking skills, but Cat pointed to Lew. Lew, looking so like his father as he did so, blushed with equal parts pleasure and embarrassment at the shouted accolades for the offering.

The next things arriving from the kitchen were bowls (mismatched, of course) of steaming, hearty beef and vegetable soup. Martha and PJ were served at the counter, where they'd been standing sipping wine.

"How in the world did you pull this off?" Martha asked PJ.

"Well, I must say the decorating was my inspiration, but the food was all Hannah. She spent twenty minutes raiding the fridge and pantry, and came up with the idea of a giant pot of soup. She talked Lew into some bread to go along with it, and the liquor just rounds things out. We've got Octavius to thank for that."

Raising her cup, Martha toasted the bookseller from afar. Smiling, he raised his plastic cup and bowed his head slightly in answer.

Shara and Hannah went around the room with shredded parmesan to add to the soup and everyone grew quiet for the first time as they dug into their dinner. The wine flowed, silver-ware clinked on dishes, and peace reigned.

For now.

Dessert was s'mores, creatively put together with supplies the campers, Helen and Don had contributed, and coffee (*Rufous Blend—always the right choice for after dinner*). Hershey's bars, Reese's cups, boxes of graham crackers and bags of marshmallows littered the counter. Jason went across the square to snap sticks off of the downed tree and handed them out for marshmallow roasting. The shop was a bustle of activity as people went out to the bonfire to prepare their s'mores, take in some snowless air and stroll around the square, then come back in and stop off at the kitchen to give thanks to the chefs. Even though the snow had ceased, in the extreme cold, the trampled sidewalks and street around the square had developed a layer of ice. Most of the strollers moved in pairs, mutually balancing through linked arms.

Martha warmed her hands over the steadily burning bonfire, enjoying the afterglow of wine, food, coffee and conversation. Ethel Jean had just finished comparing Margaret, dressed in black and toasting her marshmallow, to the Grim Reaper tending the flames of Hell when raised voices attracted Martha's attention.

"You have some nerve, saying that to me!" a woman's voice yelled from Birds 'n' Beans. Hurrying back to the shop, Martha arrived just in time to hear a male voice respond.

"It's true, and you know it. You have plenty of reason to want to hurt Benjamin." Scott Murphy was red-faced and yelling at Shara Yang across the shop. "I recognized you right away from all of your social media rants about Benjamin. I've seen your Facebook posts where you tried to smear him to cover your own rear end," he said. "You should be ashamed of yourself."

"He may be like a god to some, but to me he was nothing. NOTHING! I didn't *care* enough about that man to want to kill him." Shara rose from her seat, swaying slightly. Before Martha had gone out to the bonfire, Shara had been relaxing with PJ and Hannah after the frantic activity of serving the food, and from the sound of her voice, the glass of wine in her hand was not her first.

Don and Helen came in with the other two women campers. They looked as confused and shocked as Martha felt.

"What's going on?" she asked, looking back and forth from Murphy to Shara.

"This woman is full of it," Murphy replied. "I still say we don't have to look any further to find Benjamin's killer. She's standing right there! Benjamin caused her to lose everything, and then she shows up in the same place where he was murdered? That *can't* be a coincidence."

"Scott, I'm not sure you're one to be throwing stones, under the circumstances," said Fred Allen, who had been nursing a cup of coffee at one of the nearby tables. "In some ways, the best thing to happen to you is Benjamin passing away. That book of yours might actually get some interest now."

"How *dare* you." Murphy's voice was venomous. "You have no idea how important this book is to me and my family. I wouldn't do anything to jeopardize it. That woman," he said, pointing at Shara Yang again, "she doesn't have anything left, thanks to Benjamin."

He stomped to the counter and refilled his wine cup, then nodded his head in Fred Allen's direction. "And what about you, Fred? From what I can tell, you were nothing better than Benjamin's lackey. Whenever he needed money, or needed bailing out, you came running like a little puppy."

He turned to Hannah. "Even you. You may be a kid, but I heard someone say you hated Benjamin because of his fossil fuel involvement. How well does anyone know you? Everyone knows environmental people can be extremists. Has anyone even *questioned* you? This backward town is a joke. I can't wait to write about it in my book. You can kiss any other tourist trade goodbye."

He fumed out of the shop, heading in the direction of the bonfire. Hannah ran into the kitchen crying with PJ trailing behind. Martha walked over to Shara and encouraged her to sit back down. Helen and Don joined them.

"Shara, what is he so worked up about?" asked Martha. "What does he mean? I thought you said you barely knew Benjamin Marshall. Is Scott maybe confusing you with someone else?" She fell quiet, hoping the small woman would feel the need to fill the silence. Eventually, Shara exhaled deeply from her mouth, making her bangs fly up.

"I wasn't totally truthful earlier. I did know Marshall pretty well, but not in a good way. I told you I am a retired faculty member, but the reason I'm retired is because of Marshall. I did meet him at a conference, and once we started talking, we realized we had a lot in common. We liked big ideas. He promised to donate a gift to my college—a named building, for heaven's sake! But at the eleventh hour, he backed out"—here, she raised her hands to form air quotes—"saying he was thinking of establishing a 'significant ornithological initiative' that would require the money he'd previously committed. He funded a minor scholarship instead, but it was a huge embarrassment to my college and my dean, and a year later, I was pushed out through a retirement incentive. I'd planned to work another ten years, and then travel the world, but thanks to Marshall, I stopped working too early to get enough money together. Now my travel is limited to camping in state parks." She laughed at the terrible irony. "I suppose I *did* hate Marshall, when you come right down to it, but I wouldn't kill him."

The party had definitely come to an end. When Helen and Don decided to head their group—including Shara—back to the campground, Martha slumped on one of the stools at the counter, her mind reeling from the finger-pointing session she'd witnessed. And it seemed the drama wasn't over. Hannah, coat and hat in hand, came rushing back out of the kitchen, angry tears still streaming down her face, and went straight out the door and into the night. PJ had just come from the kitchen in pursuit of Hannah when Frank and Mary Jane came into the shop. From the smear of chocolate on Mary Jane's face, Martha guessed she'd been hard at work attacking a s'more.

"What in the world happened?" Frank said, looking from Martha to PJ. "We just saw Hannah come running out of here, but she kept going when we called to her."

"Murphy had too much to drink and was going on about all the people who had grudges against Marshall and might be responsible for his murder," Martha said.

PJ added, "The idiot said something about Hannah not liking the guy because of his fossil fuel investments and suggested she might be some kind of an environmental terrorist."

"WHAT?" cried Frank, anger flashing in his eyes. "My daughter's no more a—"

"We know, we know," said PJ in a calming voice. "She's just a kid, trying to find her way in life and thinking some really deep thoughts. I was starting to get through to her earlier today, and now Murphy drops this bomb. It just set her off and out she went."

Frank ran back out to the bonfire and Martha could see him gesticulating to the group gathered there. Some were pointing, Martha guessed in the direction they'd seen Hannah run. Several of them broke off and headed with Frank in that direction.

This was the second time a search group had been organized in as many days. Martha looked up, silently praying that this group's result would be very different than that of the first.

Chapter Fourteen

PJ shifted from cleaning up the dinner remnants to making coffee. *Gotta be Italian Roost*, Martha thought, reflecting that the coffee selection was starting to become second nature for her. Fred Allen, Pastor Pat and Ellie came back in and picked up where PJ had left off on the cleanup.

"Frieda went along on the search," Fred said to Martha, reading the question in her eyes. "She's got the best night vision on the planet and is good in difficult terrain. I'm no use in the dark."

"Really?" Pat said. "Sounds like she's done time in the service."

"Far from it," Fred said. "She accompanied me on some of my trips to Africa and South America, and we were lucky enough to do things like tromp through rainforests and go on safaris."

"I'm going to go help with the search too. Do we know who's out there already?" Martha asked as she suited up in her winter clothes.

"Frank, Mary Jane, Ethel Jean, Jason, Dennis, Carl, Lew, and Frieda, I think," Fred said. That meant that the older pairs—Octavius and Margaret, and Jimmy and Delores—must already have gone home and be safely tucked away for the evening. There was no sign of Ana, but Martha guessed the young woman had probably slipped back upstairs when the argument about who might have murdered her father, and why, flared up in the shop.

Martha finished putting her winter gear on, then turned to look at PJ.

"I've got it. You go," he said. Martha nodded and headed out with the store's hefty Maglite in hand.

Though the snow had stopped, the bitter cold had deepened. Martha strapped on her snowshoes, not certain where to go first. She could hear distant voices yelling, but since there was no movement in the square, she decided to look at the rear of the shops. Skating along at a good pace atop the icy snow, silently thanking Jason for loaning her the snowshoes, she shined the light all around, checking behind dumpsters and calling for Hannah at the top of her lungs.

Where would a twenty-year-old woman go in these temperatures? Had anyone even checked Frank's place to make sure she hadn't gone there? Snowshoeing around to the front of the shops again, Martha glided up to the hardware store, then around to a side door she knew was a separate entrance up to Frank's loft above the shop. She pounded on the door and, to her surprise, heard footsteps descending the stairs.

The door was flung open to reveal Mary Jane, chocolate still streaking her anxious face and staticky hair standing on end.

"Any sign of her?" Martha asked.

"Nothing. Frank asked me to stay here in case she came back. He told me he was going to get the snowmobile out to go and look for her."

"OK," Martha said. "I'll keep an eye out, but I think I'll stay close to the square. Sounds like others are branching out further. We've got to find her soon. It's too cold for her outside without any shelter."

Mary Jane reached out and squeezed one of Martha's gloved hands. "We've *got* to find her. Frank..." She trailed off, unable to articulate what she had been about to say. Martha guessed the gist of it.

"I know," she said. She might not have had children, but she could imagine how she would feel if Penny was out there somewhere in the frigid night.

She moved back out into the square, gliding past the embers of the bonfire and to the end by Toad in a Hole. A movement caught her eye, and she looked up to see Octavius and Margaret in the picture window, waving their arms.

"Not now, guys, I don't have time to visit," she mouthed, pointing to her watch and shaking her head in the negative. But Margaret gestured to her to wait a minute and made frantic motions to Octavius, who disappeared. Martha signaled back to Margaret that she needed to keep going, but Margaret put her hands together into a praying gesture, begging her to wait for a moment.

Octavius came back with a thick marker and a pad of paper. Margaret snatched it from him and scribbled something, holding it up. Martha could make out the words *FRANK GARAGE.*

Martha shrugged her shoulders. What about Frank's garage? Margaret scribbled again.

GO!

Martha knew Frank's garage was in the rear of his building, but she couldn't figure out why the elderly pair wanted her to go there and was borderline irritated at their interference when she was in the midst of a serious situation. She hadn't checked it before since it was hidden behind a couple of other outbuildings, but she figured she could swing round there, have a quick look, and then come back to the front of the shops to keep an eye out for Hannah.

Waving and nodding to Margaret and Octavius, she followed her previous track to return the way she had come. From the back of the hardware store, she snowshoed down a narrow alley between two brick garages and came out onto a small street. The door of the garage where Frank kept his truck and snowmobile was down, but the light was on inside and she could hear an engine running.

That's weird, she thought.

"Frank? Hannah?" Martha called as she removed a glove and banged on the door. Nothing.

Moving to the window on the side of the garage, she brushed away some crusted snow and looked in. The garage was misty with exhaust fumes, but she could make out a figure slumped over the truck's steering wheel. Taking off her snowshoes, she ran to the garage door and heaved it back on its metal tracks. Clouds of exhaust roiled out, so Martha breathed into the arm of her coat as she made her way to the driver's side door. She flung it open.

Martha struggled to pull Frank's heavy body out of the seat and onto the cement floor of the garage. She lowered his head down gently, then grabbed both booted feet to drag him out of the garage and into the snowy street. Laying him out flat, she left him momentarily while she tugged the keys from the ignition, then ran right back and crouched next to him, pulling off her gloves and shaking his shoulders.

"Frank! Frank!" she yelled into his face, but couldn't rouse him. The snow under him turned dark and Martha felt around the back of his head. As she held up her hand in the moonlight, her stomach heaved at what was on it; blood.

As she was loosening his scarf and coat to check for a heartbeat, Mary Jane yelled from the alley.

"Martha? What's going on?"

"It's Frank!" Martha exclaimed. "Hurry! I found him in the truck with the motor on and the garage door closed. I don't know how long he was unconscious. I think someone hit him on the back of the head." She held up her bare hand to show Mary Jane the blood that was smeared on it.

"Nonononono," Mary Jane moaned, falling down into a crouch next to Martha and pushing her roughly aside. Feeling for a pulse along Frank's neck, Mary Jane then did something bizarre; she rubbed his face with snow. Then she started slapping him. Martha just watched, not sure if it was a medical procedure or panic her friend was displaying.

Nothing happened.

Just as Martha began to think it was time to pull Mary Jane away, Frank heaved himself up, coughing and gasping for air. Then he turned his head just in time to projectile vomit across the snowy drive rather than all over Mary Jane. He put his hand on the back of his head and winced.

"Hannah," he said gruffly. "She's gone."

Between them, Martha and Mary Jane got Frank back to the shop and up the stairs to his loft. Martha had never been inside and was surprised to see an immaculate open-plan design with exposed brick and beams. After they'd helped him onto the couch, Martha rummaged in the cabinets for a strong drink while Frank told them what happened.

"I was with the others for a short bit, but then I told Mary Jane to go back to my apartment while I got the snowmobile out to look for Hannah. The snowmobile was gone, but I don't know if it was her or someone else that took it. I thought I'd try the truck, even though I didn't think it would make it far in this snow, and the last thing I remember was reaching for the handle to open the door." He felt the back of his head and closed his eyes with pain.

"Somebody knocked you out," said Martha, "and they tried to kill you by putting you in the truck and leaving the ignition on with the garage door closed." She looked up at Mary Jane. "You stay here. I've got to go warn the others."

"You can't go out there on your own," Frank objected, standing and swaying dangerously on his feet. Mary Jane helped him back down onto the couch.

"Honey, I don't want to leave you, but like you said, we can't let Martha go out there alone," she told him. "We'll lock up behind ourselves and send someone back to sit with you."

Frank was in no position to argue and he knew it. "Go," he said, "but at least take some kitchen knives with you. And tell the others we need to find Hannah." His eyes welled up with tears of frustration and fear for his daughter.

The two women each grabbed a knife from the kitchen block and Mary Jane snatched Frank's keys from the counter. Out the door they went, locking it behind them.

When they emerged from around the corner of the shops, as Martha had hoped, most of the search party had assembled in the square. They'd banked up the bonfire again. Martha yelled to them as she and Mary Jane approached.

"Has anyone seen Hannah, or anyone else for that matter, on Frank's snowmobile?" A set of stunned faces stared back at her.

Carl spoke first. "No sign of her or the snowmobile. We've all been together here for the last several minutes. Why, what's happened?"

Martha told the searchers as succinctly as she could what had happened to Frank, watching as surprise turned to shock on their faces. What no one said—they didn't need to—was that before the group had assembled back in the square, they'd been running all over the village. Any one of them could have been Frank's attacker.

"We need to keep on looking for Hannah," she said. "She's so vulnerable out in these temperatures..." Martha broke off, not wanting to voice the fact that there was a killer on the loose. Instead, she added, "Someone needs to go sit with Frank."

"I will go tend to Frank until you return," said Carl.

"You'll need to help him into a hot bath, and then get him into bed," said Mary Jane. The tall German just nodded.

Jason looked at Martha. "There's nothing more we can do tonight," he said sadly. "And the later it gets, the more exhausted we'll get, so the lower our chances of finding Hannah and figuring out who attacked Frank. I suggest we all get home, but everyone sleep in a room where you can lock your door. We don't know who attacked Frank or killed Benjamin, but the likely culprit is standing right here." Subtlety and exhaustion clearly didn't go hand in hand. "Lock your doors, folks. That's the only way we can guarantee our safety tonight."

Before anyone could respond, Scott Murphy came running out of the shop, arms flying.

"My laptop! Where is it? Did one of you move my laptop?" He frantically grabbed around in his coat pocket. "My backup drive. It's gone too!" He looked from person to person. "Which one of you took it? My book is on it and it's my *entire life*!" He actually started to cry, causing some in the group to look away.

Looking at Martha, Scott continued, "PJ says he didn't see anyone come into the shop because he—she—um... was in the back, washing dishes most of the time. How could she have not *heard* anyone?"

Jason walked over to the distraught man. "Scott, no one knows where your laptop is, but I promise you, you'll have better luck finding it in the morning." To the group, he said, "Everyone, head home, and in the morning we'll make sense of what's happened here tonight. Anyone who needs a ride, I'll take you in my truck. Scott, instead of going to look after Frank with Carl, or returning with Lew to An Early Riser, why don't you ride with me for now? We'll help get these folks home. Then we can stop by the police station and give Officer Daniels his to-go plate and an update. He probably still can't leave the station, but we can at least tell him everyone except Hannah is home safe and sound for now."

As Carl turned to walk in the direction of Frank's hardware store, he mouthed a "Thank you" to Jason.

The group broke up, some climbing into Jason's truck and some walking home in pairs or small groups. Martha tried to read their faces, but most were part red from the heat of the bonfire and part slack from the shock of the evening's events.

What is happening? Is anyone safe? And most concerning of all: *Where is Hannah?* With Officer Daniels unable to leave the police station, it was up to Martha to start putting the pieces together before someone else got hurt.

Chapter Fifteen

Finally, the square was empty apart from Martha and Mary Jane. The last view Martha had of Scott, he was scrunched down in his coat against Jason's truck's passenger door, looking like a pouting child who had just been told it was time for him to stop playing and go home for a nap.

The dying bonfire could no longer hold off the cold, so Martha and Mary Jane headed for the shop. PJ had left to take Ana home.

"I don't think I can drink any more coffee," said Martha to Mary Jane. "But would you like some?"

"Yes, I ought to drink one more cup. I know it's too late and cold to go back out looking for Hannah, but if you don't mind leaving the shop lights on, at least she'll see that someone's here if she returns in the middle of the night. I really should get back to Frank, though."

"It's totally fine to leave our lights on, and we can sit here for a bit and see if she comes back," Martha said, pouring Mary Jane a coffee from the still-hot urn PJ had left. "And I think it might be best if you let Carl get Frank settled, at least for now. He might rest better without you hovering. You and I can keep our eyes out for Hannah just as easily here."

"I just don't understand what's happened to our village," said Mary Jane, blowing on the hot coffee in the mug Martha had given her. "Who in the world would try to kill *Frank*, for heaven's sake? He's never hurt a fly. It's *got* to have been one of these hikers or campers. When I find out who it was, I'm going to..." Her voice trailed off, but Martha saw something fierce in Mary Jane's eyes that made her glad her friend had not finished her sentence.

She reached over and squeezed Mary Jane's hand. "We've got to figure it out before anyone else gets hurt," she said. "In forty-eight hours, we've gone from someone being murdered in the night to another person almost being killed out in the open, and now we have a young woman missing. It feels like whoever is doing this, their actions are escalating. Since we've agreed to sit here and see if Hannah makes her way home, what do you say to us going through some possibilities?" When they'd put their heads together earlier in the fall, Mary Jane had helped Martha clarify some of her jumbled impressions. Maybe she would do the same now.

"If you have any extra Hershey bars left over from those s'mores, you're on," Mary Jane said, nodding. Martha shuffled through the leftover ingredients and found an open Hershey's bar with several serviceable squares of chocolate still intact. She handed it to Mary Jane and her friend's eyes perked up just a bit.

Martha strode over to the rack near the front door that held free maps of local hikes and area wildflower and bird checklists. She selected a bird checklist, walked over to snatch a pen from behind the cash register, and returned to sit next to Mary Jane. Flipping over the checklist to its blank side and licking the tip of her pen, she said the words she'd been dreading having to speak.

"I hate to say this, but I think we have to start with the obvious suspect for Benjamin's murder: Hannah."

Mary Jane opened her mouth to object, but then stopped herself and said, "I know you're right. Frank would be upset at the mere suggestion that she's involved in something untoward, but you taught me in the fall that we can't leave anyone out if we are going to do this investigating murder thing right. Where should we start looking for evidence?"

Martha thought about it. "Why not start right at the beginning?" she said, jotting notes. "The first time I learned of any connection between Hannah and Benjamin was when Jason and I overheard Hannah and Frank having words. She'd been out and came back late on the snowmobile the night Marshall was killed. We heard her saying something to her dad about how Marshall's death was probably good for the whole planet, that he'd invested in fracking and Big Bad Birds had caused some endangered species' habitats to become even more fragile. She seemed genuinely glad that the man had been killed."

Mary Jane looked at Martha, her mouth hanging open just a bit. "Go back. Did you say Hannah had been out on Frank's snowmobile that night? Before or after Marshall had been found?"

"Both," Martha said miserably. "Frank said he heard her go out and return the night Marshall went missing, I don't know exactly when, and she also went out the next day. She got back just as we were all heading home after the bonfire in honor of Marshall."

"Yeah, I know Frank was worried about her going out on the snowmobile the day we found Marshall's body. So, what you're saying, in other words, is we can't account for Hannah's whereabouts at the time of Marshall's murder *and* she was overheard saying she didn't care if he was dead. And now she's missing."

"Yes. I wasn't sure if you or Frank had put those pieces together yet. I'd made the connection earlier, but had hoped we'd find the real murderer before we had to look at Hannah as a possible suspect." Martha sighed miserably. "Mary Jane, I'm sure she had nothing to do with any of this, but we have to keep thinking to figure out who did."

Mary Jane nodded anxiously, placing a final square of chocolate in her mouth. "Who's next?" she garbled.

Martha wrote down Scott's name on her paper and drew a line under it. "How about Murphy? He's a strange bird," she said.

"He's definitely got some issues."

"We know he's writing a book about Marshall. And I learned from Delores today that his first two books were *unauthorized* biographies of celebrities, which apparently were panned by reviewers and I'm guessing didn't sell very well. This book was going to be his first *real* biography, which was why he was trailing after Marshall."

"I can offer a bit more about him; I spoke to Cat earlier. She had asked him if there was anyone at home who would be worried about him, making casual conversation, and he spilled that he has a wife and two children. Apparently, his boy has special needs and his condition is getting to the point where his wife will need to quit her job to care for him full time. There's a lot of pressure on Murphy to finish this book and for it to be a financial success."

They both absorbed this for a moment. Then Mary Jane raised her hands and shrugged.

"I just don't see how killing his subject could benefit him in any way."

A memory tugged at Martha's mind. "Wait a minute. When I was over at the bookshop earlier, talking to Octavius and Margaret, she joked about her first book selling better if something terrible happened to her. And Fred Allen said something similar when the big blowup happened after dinner."

Once again, the two women sat quietly.

"You know, I think there may be something to that," Mary Jane said at last. "This isn't very nice of me, but when a famous author passes away, I sometimes think it's a good time to finally read their books. But when I try to check them out of the library, I often have to place them on a hold because everyone else has had the same idea. Perhaps it's the same thing with biographies—when the subject dies, there's suddenly a spike in interest in them. In that case, Scott's book sales might be higher with Marshall's death."

She gave an involuntary shudder at the thought. Martha kept writing.

"But where does the stolen laptop come in?" Mary Jane continued. "I think we both know that Murphy didn't misplace it, or his backup drive. That laptop's the one thing he actually seems to care about and it never leaves his side. Is someone trying to make sure he doesn't publish that book for some reason?"

"That's what I'm thinking. Is there something in the book that would point out our murderer?"

"But how would that connect to someone trying to kill Frank? He has no idea what Murphy wrote in the book and no connection to Marshall whatsoever."

"The pieces are still not fitting. Let's keep going on our list. How about Fred?"

Mary Jane talked while Martha scribbled. "What do we know about Fred? He seems like such a nice man, and his wife seems nice as well. I'm not sure I see where they fit in at all as suspects."

Martha tapped her paper. "Well, I've jotted them down, but I'm not sure they fit in either. Here's what I know from chatting with them while they worked at the library: Fred and Marshall attended business school in Cambridge, Massachusetts, and that's where they met. They went their separate ways, had their separate successes, and somehow reconnected through an alumni event. Since then, the Allens have invested in some of Marshall's projects. It sounds like Fred was the steady friend of the two men, sometimes bailing Marshall out of trouble. There's nothing I've heard that would cause either Fred or Frieda to harm Marshall. Unless..."

Mary Jane sat to attention. "What?" she asked eagerly.

"When we were first at the church and Tanner was giving Frank and me a brief run-down of the hiking group, he told us the Allens had lost a hefty sum on one of their investments with Marshall and there was some bad feeling for a time after. The funny thing is that neither Fred nor Frieda ever mentioned that. If I'd lost a ton of money, I suppose I might have remembered it."

"Could it be that the old saying 'Never speak ill of the dead' kept them from mentioning it?"

Martha nodded. "Good point," she said. "Or it could be they don't want anyone to know they fell out with Marshall at one point." She looked down at her paper. "OK," she said, making a few notes, "now let's talk about Dennis Tanner."

"Kind of hard to pin him down," Mary Jane said, nodding. "Sometimes he seems the devoted number two to Benjamin, but he has a certain edge that makes it not quite believable."

"Wow, Mary Jane, you have good instincts. Ana actually told me that the first thing Tanner said to her after they found out that Benjamin was dead was that she could scrap the Center project."

"Cold," Mary Jane said, shaking her head. "But would he actually harm the guy he'd worked for all these years just to get him to scrap a business deal? Hadn't he seen tons of business deals come and go? What was so special about this one that would make it worth killing over?"

"I can answer that. Marshall was going to sell off a collection of old books and stuff. Illuminated manuscripts and the like. Yeah, don't ask," Martha said, seeing the obvious question on Mary Jane's face. "Marshall wanted to use the library they're all housed in for part of his bird research center, making it the largest in the world, so he was going to divvy the books and papers up between other collections, but Tanner was furious. He says it's the collection in its entirety that makes it so rare, it's priceless. It even contains a literary gem Tanner himself discovered years ago." Martha pondered for a moment. "Who knows how far the man would go to save the Stedman collection? But murder? I'm not sure I see it either. To be honest, so far, Hannah seems like the strongest possibility."

Mary Jane shook her head. "You're forgetting the women at the campground," she said.

Martha wrote down their names. "Fair enough. Only one of them, Shara Yang, has a connection to Marshall. And what's more, just a bit ago, I found out from Shara that that connection is not so distant as she'd first suggested. Marshall ruined her career and forced her into a retirement that is not so easy financially."

"Is that enough to kill someone over? And how could she have even gotten out to the pond?" Mary Jane asked.

"I've thought about that. Academics can be a strange breed. Their reputation is everything to them, and the fiasco at Shara's college sounds like it brought some really bad attention her way, ending with her forced retirement. Maybe that *was* enough to kill him over. Plus, Don leaves the keys in his POV—his privately owned vehicle."

Mary Jane nodded impatiently and Martha realized she probably already knew that.

She went on, "What if Shara drove it down to the pond and killed Marshall?" Martha looked at Mary Jane, waiting to see if she'd created a plausible story, then spotted the holes in it all by herself. "Hmmmm, that doesn't work. She somehow lured Marshall out of the church into the middle of nowhere, without anyone else seeing, and used a gun she just *happened* to have on her to shoot him."

"The same questions could be posed about Hannah, though, right?" Mary Jane countered. "How could she have gotten Benjamin to come out of the church and to the pond?"

Both women were quiet for a few minutes, gazing out to the square in troubled concentration.

"There's someone we haven't talked about," Martha said, looking down at a name she'd just spelled out. "Ana."

Mary Jane drew back, head cocked as if questioning Martha's sanity. "Benjamin's own *daughter*?"

"Mary Jane, we have to consider everyone. In fact, if we really were detectives, we'd probably even consider villagers. In this case, though, as far as we know, no one from the R-C knew Benjamin or had any connection to him. So let's leave them out for the moment, but we do have to at least consider Ana."

As if on cue, PJ hurried through the front door.

"I forgot to take a few things out of the freezer to thaw in the fridge for tomorrow. We have no idea how long we're going to be cooking for everyone. Don't let me interrupt you." PJ made a beeline to the kitchen and the two women could hear the freezer door opening and closing. Other kitchen sounds continued as Martha turned back to Mary Jane.

"Ana," she said resolutely.

"OK," Mary Jane said. "First, what in the world would be her motive?"

Martha sighed. "Well actually, she's got a couple. First off, she told me herself that Marshall left his entire estate to her. But she did seem genuinely surprised at having learned that from Tanner at the church after we'd found Benjamin's body. If she hadn't known he'd planned to leave her everything, then that's not a very strong motive."

"What is the other motive?" Mary Jane asked. "I haven't really talked too much to her."

"She shared with me that she'd really disliked him, which stemmed from some resentments she had about how she'd been raised. But it sounded to me like she'd gotten past that recently and was starting to rethink her relationship with him."

"But, Martha, we've been wrong before about people. Remember Mavis?"

Ugh. How could I forget the woman who nearly killed me?

"True enough. But why would Ana choose to kill him out here? She could probably think of a million ways for him to die back in the city—ways that would never be traced back to her. And being his sole heir is almost too obvious a motive. She's a smart woman and knows the police would look to her first."

As they pondered the many conflicting facts surrounding their suspect list, PJ rang the call bell that sat on the counter of the window cutout between the shop and the kitchen. She had a strange, unsettled look on her face.

"What is it, PJ?" Martha asked.

Gulping, eyes large, PJ raised a hand. In it was a small tea towel, and in the towel lay a hard, glinting black gun.

"I'm guessing that thing on the end that looks like a Hostess Ho Ho is a silencer," Martha said, adrenalin fueling her bad joke.

"Where in the world did you find *that*?" Mary Jane asked. Both she and Martha stood up and hurried over to the cutout.

"In the drawer next to the stove. Right where... right where both Shara and Hannah were prepping food."

"But you can't think that—"

"Honey, I don't think anything. People have been in and out of the shop most of the day. Just about anyone could have put that there."

Martha shivered. "Don't you see what this means? The killer was *here*. He was right in here with us, and the hikers, and the campers, and he could have hurt any one of us."

"Or she," PJ said.

"Huh? Oh yes, or she," Martha said. "I don't like this one bit. The killer, whoever they are, is getting closer to the village center. If the same person who put this gun in the kitchen also stole Murphy's laptop, they don't seem very afraid of being caught."

Mary Jane looked at them and said in a low voice, "Or they are getting desperate. Remember what Mavis did?"

Martha didn't need to answer. Of course she remembered. They all did. A murderer who feels threatened goes to any lengths to protect themselves and their secrets.

She felt fire flood her thoughts. "Then we have to make sure we don't make the same mistake twice. We can't wait for the mountain to come to Mohammed."

Martha had just one chance to catch the killer. She had to make it count.

Chapter Sixteen

Morning dawned crisp and cold, but with no additional snow accumulation. Martha went downstairs and busied herself in the shop, brewing fresh coffee and refilling the cream, milk, and half and half located at the self-serve bar. She'd taken extra time deciding on what coffee to serve this morning, and settled on Birder Blend. After all, she'd be taking a hike of sorts a bit later, and what could be better beforehand?

She stood up straighter, willing her brain to catch up with her body's confident pose. Setting out the filled urns, she pumped fresh coffee into a "Nice Tits" mug, poured a splash of cream in it, and took it upstairs to Jason. He was awake when she came in and sat up on his cot to receive the mug. Taking a satisfied slurp, he looked at the side of the cup.

"Nice tits?" he said questioningly.

"Certainly," Martha said primly. "You've got your marsh tit, willow tit, blue tit... even your bearded tit." As she said the last one, she reached out and gently tugged at the bottom of Jason's own ginger beard. "All very nice tits." With an innocent shrug, she turned to go back downstairs. "More coffee where that came from whenever you get up. I'm going to buzz everyone and let them know to come on over when they and their hikers are ready to eat something."

She began to feel energized and just a tad mischievous, knowing she was one step ahead of a killer who'd dared to try

to intimidate her and her friends. And who had almost suc-
ceeded in killing Frank. That more than anything had galva-
nized Martha into formulating a plan with Mary Jane and PJ
last night before her two friends had gone home.

He or she has messed with the wrong village, Martha
thought, clenching her fists.

She walked across the floor of the shop to the walkie-talkie
that Jason had left charging the night before. There she called
up each of the hosts, or the neighbor closest to the host who'd
been given one of the handsets. Little by little, she got the word
out to the group that coffee was on, there would be breakfast at
the shop, and they were to come on over when they were ready.

Once Martha had completed this first task she greeted PJ,
who arrived at the exact time she'd been expected.

"Do you know there are drops coming down from the edge
of the awning?" she asked with a broad smile. "Melting! It's
starting to melt! There may be an end to this mess after all."

"Oh, there will be an end to this, all right," Martha said
with a knowing glance.

After taking off all of her warm layers, PJ approached
Martha and put one of her large, bejeweled hands gently on her
forearm.

"You ready for this, honey?" she asked, sympathy and concern in her eyes. "It's not too late to call it off."

"Absolutely," Martha replied. "And step one is already in
motion. I've called everyone to come for breakfast."

"I still don't like not telling Chip or Jason," PJ said crossly.
"I don't think it's wise."

"If we tell Chip, you know he'll call it off. But we can't
wait for the roads to open and things to get back to normal;

you know that. Who can tell what else the killer might do before that happens? And once everything opens, how can we keep them from slipping away? Everyone will want to get their car out and rush out of town, resupply, call electricians and plumbers and everyone else that we'll need to put the village back together after this storm. In all of that bustle, how in the world will Chip be able to wrangle all of the hikers and campers and make them stay here so an investigation can be launched?"

PJ took a deep breath and blew it out. "When you put it like that... but can't you at least tell Jason?"

"Absolutely not. He'll want to do it himself and go all Rambo about the whole thing. This requires delicacy and tact, *not* two things he possesses in excess. No, right now, we're ahead of the killer. We want to keep it that way. They have no clue we're onto them and that we're going to catch them today."

She looked hard at PJ. "Something Ana said about blue jays keeps going around in my head. They're territorial and willing to do whatever they have to in order to get what they want. Our killer is exactly the same way. And they are going to want that jump drive. I'm counting on it."

"If I didn't know better, I'd say you're actually enjoying yourself," said PJ.

"Well, there's nothing I like better than solving a mystery, as you know." PJ was well aware of her penchant for mystery books as she and the other gals had teased Martha each time she'd returned to the shop from the Riley Creek Public Library with an armful of whodunits.

Giving up on trying to change Martha's mind, PJ set about preparing food. Carl had dropped off two boxes of baked goods while Martha had been prepping the coffee bar, so all PJ needed to do was set tables, put out coffee mugs and pitchers of juice, and turn on the warming oven.

"Popping over to Toad in a Hole. I'll be right back," Martha said, grabbing her walkie-talkie and coat. PJ looked at her through the pass-through as the cardinal sounded ten on the clock. "The cardinal is a symbol of good luck," she added, giving PJ a wink as she bounded out the door.

"I've got a bad feeling about this," were the last words she heard from PJ before the door closed behind her.

When Martha re-entered Birds 'n' Beans, it had transformed into a bustling breakfast scene. Hikers and their hosts were sprinkled at tables all around the shop. Don had brought the three campers down from the campground and Helen was out filling the feeders in the viewing garden. Several people were gathered around Frank; from their concerned expressions, Martha guessed they were still processing the news from last night. There was a buzz in the room which Martha sensed stemmed in equal parts from shock about the previous evening's events, concern over Hannah still being missing, and growing anticipation around the second search Frank was suggesting to everyone he spoke to. One or two villagers, Margaret and Octavius in particular, were also expressing concern about the fact no one had seen or heard from Tara Jackson since the storm began.

It was time for Martha to jump into action before everyone finished talking and left to start the search. She caught Mary Jane's eye and the older woman gave her a barely perceptible nod. Mary Jane had been quietly separating the hosts from the others for private conversations as she moved around the shop, apparently inviting them to watch a bird in the viewing area, or to help in the kitchen, or to look at something upstairs.

The Allens were looking at the binocular display, Fred showing interest in the high-end Swarovskis.

Boy, I'd love to make that sale. Martha berated herself for thinking about profits at a time like this. *But still, I'd love to make that sale.*

PJ seemed to enjoy running around playing hostess, and Martha noted that she'd donned her special occasion gingham apron with ruffles that ran along the shoulders. But when she caught her eye, Martha recognized an edge of nervousness. Jimmy and Delores sat at a table with Pastor Pat, Ellie and Scott Murphy. Ellie was speaking animatedly to Pat and Jimmy. Murphy looked a bit better than the night before, but not by much. Delores was turned toward him, a sympathetic expression on her face as he no doubt poured out his misery about the missing laptop.

Jason came down the stairs and walked into the center of the shop, coffee cup in hand. "Hey, everyone, I just got off the walkie-talkie with Chip Daniels. He was able to get through on the satellite phone this morning and it sounds like the last trees will be out of the way by this afternoon. The storm moved off and we'll be getting some help soon."

"Damn. And I was just beginning to enjoy myself," Ethel Jean shouted back. She'd been seated with Tanner, and Martha caught the grin the two exchanged after Ethel Jean's outburst.

I'll be damned. Martha shook her head. *Looks like Ethel Jean made a friend.*

Martha joined Don and Jason near the counter, not missing the questioning glances she was getting from the hosts and Mary Jane. She gave them all a curt nod of her head.

We're still a go.

Don had a big grin on his face. "Finally. I think folks are starting to go stir crazy. To be honest, I know Helen and I are."

"Absolutely, it's great news," Martha said. She hated not being totally honest with her friends, but to pull this off, she needed to stick to the game plan. Voices of relief sounded among the hikers and campers, who all wanted to get packed up so they'd be ready to go once the roads opened. Some began to trickle out onto the sidewalk, splashing into the slush that just last night had been solid ice. Several of them had pulled out their cell phones and were holding them up in the air in hopes that they'd get a signal. Scott Murphy's shaking head as he walked away from the shop told Martha what she needed to know. Still nothing.

Good. Just the way I want it.

Martha made a show of telling Helen she was going up to the office to get something. When she came down, Carl Shipman and his wife Cat were sitting nearest the door. The table right next to them held Shara and the other two campers.

"I'm headed to the police station," she said, leaning in as if telling just the Shipmans, but making sure her voice projected enough so Shara could hear it. "I found a flash drive in the shop last night. I'm thinking it must be Scott's and fell out of his coat. If the murderer stole his laptop, there might be something incriminating on this. I'm going to get it over to Chip so he can take a look at it."

Carl asked if she wanted him to go with her, or even instead of her. Martha recognized that his offer was meant to give her a last chance to ditch the plan.

"No." Martha said it a bit too quickly. "No, thank you, Carl. I think I could use the exercise. Without any trail running or bowling practice, I'm starting to regain my freshman fifteen." She patted her stomach, donned her coat and hat, made eye contact with all of the hosts she could see inside, and headed out the door. It took everything she had not to turn around as she left the square. She was counting on the hosts already outside seeing her make a beeline across the square. As planned, they would then casually mention her "discovery" and her destination to their guests.

Looking up to her left, she saw Margaret and Octavius in the picture window above Toad in a Hole. They waved to her with coffee mugs in hand. Octavius had a set of binoculars around his neck and gave her a thumbs up.

So far, so good.

She started down the road that led from the square toward Aunt Lorna's cottage and on to the police station, the river on her left. The adrenalin coursing through her veins made her want to sprint, but she held herself to a slow pace, forcing herself to look around as if on a Sunday stroll. She'd worn her boots with no snowshoes for this reason. Conveniently, it was still slow going, even though the snow had begun to soften in the sun. As she pretended she was a tourist, taking in the simple beauty of the day, she put every ounce of her focus into her peripheral vision each time she turned her head.

Is anyone following me?

She'd walked for about ten minutes and was just passing a rundown mill that sat back from the riverbank. In some places, it was so dilapidated that Martha could see through the whole building and to the trees beyond. Although it was a skeleton of its former self, it still held a kind of rustic beauty. As she reached the far end of the building, she heard a voice call to her.

"Martha, Martha, over here!" She looked to the left, down the wall of the mill that was perpendicular to the river. At the end of the wall, just his top half showing, was Scott Murphy. He motioned to her to come to him.

Here we go, Martha thought. *Keep your cool, Sloane.*

Cautiously, she picked her way through the deep snow along the wall of the mill. Where there weren't holes in the planks, Martha could feel the slight warmth of the sun bouncing off of the wood. Where there were gaps, she spied a flock of starlings on the ground, scavenging flecks of grain.

Amazing how sharp your senses get when you're confronting a murderer.

She got to within a yard of Murphy, her heart pounding under her coat. He stepped out from behind the mill and Martha braced herself.

"Scott, what are you doing here?" she asked, trying to keep her voice breezy but hearing it shake a bit on her last word.

"I came as quick as I could when Carl told me you'd found my flash drive. Can I see it?" he asked, holding out a hand.

"Scott, I don't think that's a very good idea. It's police evidence now, since someone seems to have stolen your laptop." She heard her voice quiver again and gave a little cough, pretending to be clearing a throat tickle.

This is harder than I thought it would be.

"Is there something on the drive you want to tell me about?" The rush of the swollen river was so loud, Martha was all but yelling at the bespectacled man.

"What are you talking about?" the young man asked, his own voice raised to compete with the river. "I just want to see the drive to make sure it's mine. I wish you'd let me take a copy before you decided to give it to the police. That's my entire life on there. I *need* to see it."

He held his hand out and moved to come nearer. Martha reached inside her coat pocket.

As she was withdrawing her hand, she heard a loud THUNK! Scott looked at her, blinked twice, and fell face-down into the snow. Standing right behind him was Frieda Allen, a short length of log held in her leather-gloved hand.

"Frieda? What? Why?" Martha stammered. Her eyes went from Scott's still form to Frieda, then back again.

"Give me the jump drive," Frieda said, her low voice so different than the melodic one she'd used during their previous conversations. Only now did Martha appreciate the other woman's physical presence. Why hadn't she noticed how fit Frieda was? How had she thought she was going to pull this off? None of the villagers had followed her. She had told them not to, thinking the murderer wouldn't be able to resist approaching her, but only if they knew she was alone.

"I said, GIVE IT TO ME!" Frieda's hand flashed out and Martha could see the handle of something dark and metallic. A knife flicked out with a solid click. A switchblade.

Martha backed up a step, stumbling slightly in the snow and holding out her gloved hands in supplication. "OK, OK. I just have to get my glove off and take it out of my inside pocket." Her heart was pounding. She held up her right gloved hand and pulled the material out finger by finger, then removed the glove and put her hand into the chest pocket of her coat.

Looking up at Frieda, she took her last chance. "Officer Daniels knows, you know. I read the book last night and radioed him this morning. I downloaded a copy onto my office computer. It's all over for you already. You can kill Benjamin and you can kill me, but you're dead in the water." Martha had to keep going. "Why did you do it? Why did you shoot Benjamin? Wasn't he one of your husband's best friends?"

Martha could read a changing landscape of emotions on the other woman's face. Anger. Fear. Desperation. Anger again. Frowning, Frieda Allen looked to the left and right, and Martha braced herself.

"You just couldn't leave it alone, could you?" Frieda hissed. "One less Marshall in the world; what would it matter? His death would hit the twenty-four-hour news cycle, or maybe he'd even get forty-eight hours, but then it would fade out. Why couldn't you have let it be a random killing by a stranger that never got solved? Why couldn't you have left it *alone*?" She was crying now, tears running mascara tracks down her face.

Martha pushed, sensing Frieda was at breaking point. "Why would you shoot your husband's best friend? Why would you try to kill *Frank*, for heaven's sake?" she asked.

Frieda's head snapped up, her simmering eyes making Martha take another step back. "Because *I* am supposed to be his best friend! I am his wife, dammit. I could see it happening all over again. I'd gotten him away from silly college boy Marshall once. And what happens? In strolls Marshall again. The same man who stole my business plan was about to steal my future with Fred. And I didn't touch Frank." She seemed to tack on the last sentence as an afterthought.

Martha could barely find her voice in the face of the other woman's intense emotion, but she scratched out, "Stole your business plan? What do you mean?"

"Big Bad Birds, dammit. *That's* what I mean. We Radcliffe girls could take a few courses at Harvard back then, and so I ended up in the same 'Intro to Business' course as Benjamin. I'd thought of this great idea about a company that takes tours to see endangered species—not just to see the birds, but to improve the local economy *and* the animals' chance of protection—and I told Benjamin about it in passing. A few years ago, I hear about this revolutionary idea Benjamin has cooked up. Big Bad Birds. *My* idea. *My* business plan. *His* success."

Martha was keeping her eye on the switchblade. Frieda handled it deftly, clearly comfortable with it. Martha felt sweat pouring down her sides, but knew she had to keep Frieda talking.

"So you killed him for stealing your idea. That's totally understandable," she said, trying to sound soothing and sympathetic.

"Don't condescend to me," Frieda snapped. "Don't try to psychobabble me and be my friend to save your own skin. Do you really think I'm that gullible?" The sparkle in Frieda's eye reminded Martha of Heath Ledger's Joker. She shut up.

"I was even willing to look past that if he'd just left Fred alone. After the money he'd cost us on the last big project, I thought we were done with him. But, oh no. Not Benjamin. Out of the blue, just as we're beginning to make plans for Fred's retirement, trips to see the kids and to see the national parks together, back he came. Again. Wanting *his* piece of Fred. Well, that was too much for him to ask. I'd earned this time with Fred. The kids had. There was no way I was going to let that man get hold of him again." By now, Frieda's tears were flowing freely, as if the retelling of the story had rekindled her rage.

"It was the perfect crime. No witnesses. Out in the middle of nowhere. Then, right after I shot Benjamin, it hit me. That damned idiot Murphy had interviewed me months ago, and I'd mentioned to him about my being a pretty good shot and about Fred and I being members of a gun club. Fred's eyesight is so bad, he hangs out in the lounge while I practice. Someone would connect my shooting experience and the murder as soon as the book was published. Murphy was obviously too stupid to make the connection himself, but it would only be a matter of time before someone else did." She was quiet for a moment, then yelled, "NOW GIVE THAT JUMP DRIVE TO ME!"

Three things happened almost simultaneously. Frieda plunged forward, the switchblade outstretched toward Martha, as Martha's hand came out of her pocket and threw a fistful of nyger seed into Frieda's eyes. As Frieda screamed, the flock of starlings took flight, exiting through the closest hole in the barn wall. The seemingly endless stream of birds whizzed around Frieda like a locust swarm, combining with the seed to temporarily blind her. That was enough time for Martha to move forward, push the other woman off her feet and wrap both hands around the wrist that held the knife.

The two women fell into a heap next to Murphy's still form. *Now what?*

The answer came with a tremendous splashing that rose above the sound of the rushing river. Jason pounded up from the shore, clad in his waders and a flannel shirt. Splayed atop Frieda's struggling form, Martha yelled at him.

"What are *you* doing here? This was supposed to be a secret. I'm fine, I'm totally *fine*."

He wrested the knife from Frieda's hand, retracted the blade, and held it out to his side. Then he replied in a slow drawl.

"Yes, I can see that."

Chapter Seventeen

The next several hours were a blur. Jason and Martha between them had been able to bring Murphy around, Martha using the face slapping trick she'd watched Mary Jane perform the previous night. Then Jason radioed Don to come pick Murphy up so that Mary Jane could examine him. When Don arrived, he gave Jason a length of rope to use to tie Frieda's hands. While Don drove Murphy back to the village, together, Martha and Jason walked Frieda the rest of the way to the police station.

When they entered the station, Chip looked from Frieda to Martha to Jason with his mouth hanging open. Jason provided a heavily abridged version of events, sharing enough information to convince Chip to place Frieda in the station's lone cell. Once she was locked in, he took frantic notes as they gave him the general outline of the morning.

Martha explained, "I knew there had to be something in Scott's book that the killer didn't want made public. I honestly didn't know what it was, but I figured that, if the killer thought a copy of the jump drive had been found, we could use it to flush them out of the woodwork."

"Looks like it worked," said Chip, breaking the lead of his mechanical pencil and thumbing the top to push out more.

"Oh, it worked, all right," said Jason, gesturing with his head at Martha. "It worked so well this ridiculous woman just about got herself killed. Again."

"I was *totally* in control of the situation," Martha said, crossing her arms and raising her chin.

"You would have been, until Mrs. Allen gathered her wits and stabbed you." Jason shook his head. "You are the most—"

"OK, people, enough," said Chip, holding up his hands like a referee parting two boxers. He turned to his walkie-talkie and said into its speaker, "Pastor Pat, come in. Pastor Pat." The two men exchanged words over the radio line before Chip signed off.

"He found the laptop in Frieda's backpack, along with the flash drive."

Looking over to the cell, Martha took in Frieda Allen. She sat on a metal chair at a small metal desk, staring at the wall and looking as if she'd just lost her best friend.

Martha sat in Octavius Bennett's living room, warming up by the woodstove. Chip had lent Jason a police van to drive them both back to the village, and Jason had dropped her off at Toad in a Hole while he rode on to the church to break the news to Fred Allen that Frieda was in custody. Chip would fill in the details when he interviewed Fred as part of the larger investigation. Martha felt too drained to witness what she knew would be a gut-wrenching scene.

Margaret handed her a small glass of sherry. Even though Martha hated the stuff, she forced a sip down and had to admit that the liquid burn at least sharpened her focus.

"Thank you for having my back," she said to them both. "I knew your front window had the best view of my walk out of town. I just expected the murderer to catch up with me before I made it so far out of the square."

"Once you were out of our sight, we weren't sure what to do, so Octavius radioed Jason at the shop and told him the basic outline of your plan. He asked what direction you'd traveled, and once we'd told him, we watched out the window. He ran into his store, came out wearing hip waders, of all things, and ran off toward the river."

Octavius took over the narrative. "That was the last we saw of him until the two of you came driving back in the police van. Thank heavens you are all right. We would never have forgiven ourselves if something had happened to you."

"But I don't understand," Margaret said, worrying at a thread on her black fisherman's sweater. "Mrs. Allen shot Mr. Marshall because her husband was going to do another business deal with him?"

"No, dear," Octavius replied. "She shot him because she'd gone along with a certain kind of life for so long, with the promise of a particular payoff at the end. The idea of that payoff, that vision of what her life could finally become, being threatened pushed her beyond her limit."

"What I don't understand is what happened to Frank," Martha said. "I asked Frieda why she'd attacked him, and she denied doing it. Why would she do that? Once she'd admitted to murder, why would she lie about a garden-variety physical assault?"

An engine sounded in the distance, getting louder as it approached.

"Do you think they've opened the roads already?" Margaret exclaimed excitedly.

"I don't think so. Chip said they still had some last trees to clear and that it would be afternoon before things would open up." Martha stood at the window, looking out, and saw Frank's snowmobile come down the road and into the square, pulling up in front of the hardware store.

"I'd better go," she said quickly.

By the time she'd made it down the stairs, out the door and around the square, Frank was leaning on Mary Jane and making his way across the green from Birds 'n' Beans. He embraced Hannah once she'd stood up from the snowmobile and taken her helmet off. PJ had come along behind Frank and Mary Jane and was helping another somewhat larger figure from the snowmobile.

It was Tara Jackson!

"Thank the goddess," PJ said, throwing her arms around the tall woman. "We've been wondering about you and had no idea where you were."

"She's been with Mr. Jeremiah, just like me," cried Hannah, standing next to her father while he held an arm around her shoulders. A chorus of confused faces stared back at Hannah and Tara.

"She's right," said Tara. "I was coming back into town Monday night after meeting my sister in Nashville at our mom's house. Would you believe it, I almost made it back to Riley Creek, but my Prius hit an ice patch and I wound up in a ditch. I was too far out of town to walk home and the only shelter I was able to find was Albert's A-frame. And thank heavens because if I'd been out there ten more minutes, I honestly think I would have been in trouble."

By now, others had joined the group outside the hardware store and a jumble of voices tripped over one another, greeting Tara and Hannah, sharing how concerned people had been, and how Margaret and Octavius wanted to start a group to better connect the village businesspeople so this could never happen again. It was clearly all a bit too much for Tara to take in, as she had tears in her eyes.

It was Frank who noticed first. "Tara, what's wrong?" he asked.

"Oh, nothing," she said, "This cold weather makes my eyes water," but PJ stepped forward with a knowing look and wrapped a muscled arm around her shoulders.

"I know," she said. "I know. Just accept it and try to get used to people giving a crap about you."

"And this one," Tara said, wiping away a tear and putting an arm around Hannah, "this one came zipping up on her snowmobile when I was trying to shovel out my car last night to come back to the shop. She convinced me it was still too cold for either of us to be out, so we both stayed the night at Albert's. Another guardian angel for me."

As the villagers stood around, laughing and talking animatedly in the way that people often do once a crisis has passed and relief takes over, Martha caught Hannah pull PJ off to the side and speak closely in her ear. PJ's head jerked back and she stared intensely into Hannah's face. They conferred for a few more seconds, then rejoined the group, PJ standing behind Hannah with her hand on the younger woman's shoulder.

"Dad?" said Hannah. "Dad, I have something to tell you." The group all turned as one to Hannah as she moved closer to her father and Mary Jane. "I didn't tell you everything," she said. Frank's brow wrinkled and he started to speak, but Hannah held her hand up. "No, wait. Let me say this. You know that night I went out on the snowmobile and didn't tell you where I was going? Well, something weird happened before I came home. I'd been out just riding and trying to clear my head, and I'd gone way out by the church and that pond where they found Marshall's... body." Hannah looked down at her feet.

"It's OK, honey, just tell him what you saw," PJ encouraged softly.

"Well, see, when I rode out there, I saw two guys walking. There was one guy with a beard and another guy, pointing into the trees and pulling the bearded guy through the snow. The guy with the beard—I think that must have been Marshall—looked like he was having trouble, but the other guy forced him to keep walking. At one point, the non-bearded guy leaned over and his hat fell off, and the moonlight caught his hair. It was bright silver."

Martha did her best to keep a neutral expression.

"What happened next, honey?" Frank said encouragingly to his daughter.

Wringing her gloves in her hands, Hannah said, "Nothing, really. I didn't think anything of it until the next day when you told me Marshall had died, and then I heard he'd been murdered. Then fast forward to last night when we were feeding everyone dinner. PJ put me on the espresso machine and the silver-haired guy came up and asked me for a cappuccino. When I made it for him and put it down on the counter, he said really quietly to me to please keep it between us that he'd been out near the pond with Marshall. He said Marshall's daughter was already so upset and it would just cause a misunderstanding. I didn't really understand it at the time, but now that I've been thinking about it, and talking to Albert and Tara about it while we were at the A-frame, that seems like a really weird thing to say. And the way he said it, just smiling and chatting along, really freaked me out."

Pieces locked into place in Martha's mind. Tanner. Pointing up in the trees. The binoculars around Marshall's neck. It felt like the many times she'd drafted disparate pieces of a speech, and then pulled them together into a coherent whole. Tanner had been out on the pond with Marshall.

Martha looked at PJ. "Has anyone seen Tanner?" she asked.

"Last I saw him, he was in Silent Sisters with Ethel Jean," PJ replied in a monotone voice.

Martha glanced at Hannah, then Frank, who was looking a bit pale. "Mary Jane, Hannah, I think Frank needs to go home and lie down. PJ, Carl, Jason, will you join me please?" Without waiting for an answer, Martha made a beeline across the square, her mind alight with the picture that was forming in her head.

Tiny bells tied to the inside handle of the antique shop's door tinkled as the four entered. Ethel Jean's head appeared from behind the counter.

"Oh great. First chance I've had to get some decent work done and the entire cast of *Bonanza* walks in." Squaring her eyes at Martha, she said, "What do you want, Ben?"

Martha completely ignored Ethel Jean and walked straight to Tanner, who'd been organizing a box of old postcards at the end of the counter. He looked at Martha, then at her three companions standing at the door. He began to speak, saw the stony look in their eyes, then looked down at the postcard in his hand and placed it gently back in the box with the others.

"I gather from the looks on your faces that you've discovered my... indiscretion."

"I'd say it's more than that, wouldn't you?" Martha said drily. "We know it was you who got Marshall out on the pond that night. Hannah saw you."

"Perhaps I did. But I didn't *shoot* Benjamin," Tanner said defiantly. "I only walked out to the pond with him, but I've never even touched a gun. *Dreadful* things." He crossed his arms in front of him, shaking his head with distaste.

"But why walk out in below zero temperatures with a man his age, after the day you'd all had? What could you possibly have been doing that was so important?"

"Benjamin wanted to go for a walk. I simply obliged him," Tanner said.

"No way. Hannah said it looked like you were pulling him along, and that he was stumbling. She said you were pointing up in the trees."

Tanner was getting more agitated by the moment. "Fine. *Fine.* I led Benjamin out to the pond. He'd brought us all the way to this godforsaken wilderness to see some birds. All right, I'd show him some birds. He wanted to see that damned snowy owl so badly and I told him this might be our last chance, that once the roads opened we'd be driven back out of this hell hole. He believed me. You see, he believed *Ana* about his money and *me* about everything else."

"But you knew he was tired. We could all see that. How could you take him back out in that condition?"

Tanner's eyes flashed. "Because I wanted to rub his face in his damned *birds*. See what they could cost him. I wanted him to sit out there for a while and think on what would happen if he didn't give up his ridiculous obsession with the research center and come back to his senses."

Ethel Jean's voice sounded, this time quiet and level. "Wait a minute. Are you saying you left him out there? On purpose? In the freezing cold?"

Tanner looked down, then back up again, taking his glasses off and rubbing their lenses on the corner of his shirt.

"I left him there to think, yes," he said testily. "Just my luck that young Miss Mad Max decided to ride by on her snow machine. She and her father were too nosey by half."

"Her father?" Ethel Jean said. "What does Frank have to do with this?"

"Oh, don't pretend. I'm not an idiot. I know she told him she saw me."

"That's interesting," said Martha. "Hannah didn't tell anyone about seeing you until just five minutes ago. No one had said a word about Frank, except you. And you just gave away your motive for trying to kill him."

"I met a lot of nasty people out west," said Jason in a low voice. "But you are one evil son of a bitch." He turned to the group. "No wonder Marshall had taken off his layers; he had hypothermia." Seeing the confusion on the others' faces, he went on, "It's not unheard of for people who are freezing to death to start removing their clothes. It's called paradoxical undressing."

The group stared at Tanner as if waiting for an answer.

"I didn't mean for him to die. I just... I just wanted him to come back to his senses. I wanted him to realize this fantasy of a bird research center was nonsense and would lead to no good. Don't you see? The Stedman collection had to remain together. I've worked on that for so long, taken so much care over it. It's my life's work. Where else would I go?"

He looked from person to person, searching for a sympathetic face and finding none.

"You sick bastard. He trusted you, and you left him out there in the snow and ice to punish him," said Ethel Jean. "Get the hell out of my store."

Chapter Eighteen

The last of the massive pine trees had been cleared from the roads leading to Riley Creek and traffic began to flow. Electricity was restored to the village late Friday morning and Martha busied herself at her cottage all afternoon, emptying her fridge of spoiled food and giving the whole place a good cleaning. Penny was content to recline in her cozy doggie bed next to the fireplace as Martha moved around her.

"No matter what happens in this town, you just sleep, don't you, girl?" Martha asked the dozing terrier. In answer, Penny rolled over, eyes still closed, until her stomach faced the ceiling and her paws hung limply in the air. Martha sighed and shook her head. She wanted to get her cottage cleaned up so she could turn her attention back to getting the shop open for business.

By Saturday morning, Martha had gotten her cottage about as clean as she was going to. Leaning down over Penny, she smelled that the little dog could use a bath, but by now, she was too antsy about getting the shop back in action. She was gathering her backpack and keys when Penny ran to the front door, sitting politely and blinking her big brown eyes.

"OK, OK, you get to come along," Martha said, raising her hands in surrender. "I did leave you with Fritz for an awful long time. I'm sure that hanging out with him, and all of Delores's delicious doggie snacks, was quite a burden for you to endure." She eased the wiggling schnauzer into her fleece doggie coat—now a little tight around the tummy—and off they went.

Martha could feel a slight uptick in the temperature and trees dripped their melting snow all around her. For the first time in days, there were enough slushy spots that she could hop from one to the next and make her way along. She reached the square quickly relative to every other outdoor journey she'd taken recently.

When she entered the square, she spotted Tara Jackson on the sidewalk outside of her salon, Looking Sharp, working with Octavius Bennett. Both had shovels, and the walkway in front of the salon was almost clear. Around the square were more shovelers in front of their respective shops: Carl and Lew; Frank and Hannah; Ethel Jean and Mary Jane. PJ, Helen and Don were shoveling off the walkway by Threaded Needle.

As Martha reached Birds 'n' Beans, she heard clapping. Confused, she looked around and saw that each villager had stopped their shoveling and was now applauding in her direction. She waved in a friendly way, but wasn't sure what was going on. Penny barked excitedly at the commotion, not understanding it either, but enjoying it all the same.

When she entered Birds 'n' Beans, she let Penny off leash. Delores, Jimmy, Pat and Ellie were sitting at one table, Margaret at another drinking what looked to be her customary cup of tea and working away at her laptop.

If people only knew what kind of smut was born in this shop, Martha thought.

"What was all that about?" she asked, unraveling her scarf and laying it and her heavy coat over the back of a stool at the counter.

"That was for you." Ellie looked the happiest Martha had seen her in days.

"Why?" Martha said.

"I'd guess something along the lines of keeping Riley Creek from becoming the Unsolved Murder Capital of the Southeast," Pat answered, placing his hand in the air with each word as if reading the name up in lights.

"For heaven's sake, I just helped figure it out, that's all."

"It is true," Jimmy said quietly. "You do have a way with putting the pieces together."

"Delores, I do believe your husband just called me nosey," Martha said, winking at Jimmy.

"Martha, we have some news," Ellie said, looking anxiously at her husband. "Pat and I think we might be pregnant."

"WHAT? But that's wonderful news! I'm thrilled for you!" Martha exclaimed.

Pat reached over to take Ellie's hand. "We're heading down to the city today. One way or the other, I think it's time we moved on from Riley Creek. We need to be a little closer to a doctor, whether Ellie is pregnant or not, because if she's not, it's time to try and change that." He let out a broad grin and Ellie teared up. Happy tears this time.

"Well, how about that," Martha said, sitting back in her chair, overjoyed for her friends.

Ana came into the shop from the upstairs office. Surprisingly, she had opted to stay in Riley Creek even though the roads had reopened, holing herself up in Birds 'n' Beans' upper rooms and working away feverishly at Martha's desktop computer on goodness knows what. Scott Murphy was also still in the village, waiting for his precious laptop to be released by the police before he returned to his family, while the devastated Fred Allen, unsurprisingly, couldn't leave fast enough.

Poor man, Martha thought as she went over to greet Ana. *He seemed a genuinely nice guy.*

"How are you?" she asked the dark-haired woman.

"I am good. Really good," Ana said. "I originally borrowed your computer to check email and see what's been going on in the world. But then I saw this lying on your desk." She handed Martha a piece of paper. It was the blue jay sketch Ana had done days before. "I started thinking about what's next for me. Now that my father is gone and Tanner will be in prison soon, it's up to me to chart my next steps. I just started writing and came up with this."

She handed Martha another paper covered in typed text. Skimming it, Martha looked up.

"Are you serious? You're going to move forward with the Center?"

Ana nodded. "Yes. Not only is it a fitting tribute to my father, but it's a way to use all of the money he left me to do something good. Most of the plans are already drawn up. I'll need to attract some more investors, but thanks to my father, I know how to do that. I even talked to Scott about expanding his book to include the genesis of the Center."

"Free advertising!" Martha observed. "Now I know why he was typing so furiously the last time I saw him."

"Spoken like a true entrepreneur," Ana returned. "Yes. If the book sells well, it will only enhance interest in the work I hope will come from the Center."

The two women smiled at each other. "I just have one question," Ana said. Martha looked at her, waiting. "The Center will feature a small independent coffee shop in its lobby. Do you think I could source my coffee from Birds 'n' Beans?"

"That would be a definite YES!" yelled PJ from the kitchen. Ethel Jean, who had been eavesdropping from the corridor connecting her shop with Birds 'n' Beans, rolled her eyes and stomped through to Silent Sisters. Penny trotted after her.

"Are you *serious*?" Martha asked.

"Totally serious," said Ana. "It will take a while to get the Center built and up and going, but that way, you have plenty of time to plan, and to get your online business running like a well-oiled machine. I would love to feature coffee roasted right here in Riley Creek."

Martha exchanged looks with PJ, then with Delores and Jimmy. "You've got yourself a deal, partner," she said evenly.

That night, Martha sat under one of Aunt Lorna's quilts on her porch swing, listening to the sound of the river. Penny lay on top of the quilt, pressed against Martha's leg for warmth. After all the events of the past few days, it felt good to sit and take it all in. Was she really going to be distributing coffee to a huge research center? Yes, she was. Ana would be sending her a contract to review in a few weeks. But she still had the rest of the winter to get through financially, so her online shop really needed to deliver.

Martha looked down at Penny. "Starting tomorrow, girl, we've got our work cut out for us. We've gotta stay in business until that contract with Ana can become a reality."

It wouldn't be all work and no play, however. The gals and Martha had decided they would go ahead with their holiday party, and in a couple of days, the Birds 'n' Beans team were scheduled to be "Bowling for the Birds," to paraphrase their

"Bowling *is* for the Birds" motto. Whether or not the tournament was still on, PJ had organized an extended practice and would not budge on the point.

"We're all tight from five days of tension and we've *got* to limber up those arms," she'd insisted while scribbling and erasing on the whiteboard, revising game strategy.

Scott and Ana were leaving Riley Creek in the morning and things were going to get back to normal. *Whatever that is*, Martha thought. Three murders and one attempted murder since she'd come to Riley Creek. *What are the odds?* she wondered. Chief Teddy Perry and Officer Allison Tomlinson had gotten back from their trip Friday morning. Just as Martha was wondering when she'd get a chance to catch up with Teddy or Allison, considering how busy they—and she—were, a voice came out of the dark.

"May I join you or is this a girls only kind of affair?" Teddy Perry came close enough that the lights streaming from the cottage illuminated his face. She could see the dark stubble of the day outlined on his jaw.

"Well, hello there," Martha said, and patted the seat next to her. She'd missed his subtle smell of pine and wood smoke. "I was wondering when I might see you."

"It's been a madhouse since I arrived back in town. With all that was here waiting for me, this is the first chance I've had to come by and say hello."

"I can only imagine," Martha replied. "It was pretty wild here *before* you got home."

"So I heard," he said, looking sideways at her. She'd been waiting for this moment; she knew Teddy would chastise her for getting involved with tracking Marshall's killer.

"Look, don't even bother telling me how I shouldn't have gotten involved and how I should have left it to the police. Chip Daniels had his hands full and I couldn't just let it go until the roads opened up. All I did was help him by gathering information. He did most of the interviews on his own. After all, I am an independent person and have every right to assist law enforcement from time to time—"

"Martha," he said, reaching over and squeezing her hand, "I wasn't going to say anything except I'm glad you're OK. I know better than to tell you *anything* about how to handle yourself." He was quiet for a second. "Well, maybe I was going to say something about Jason Turngate sleeping with you at the shop, but..." He trailed off.

Martha turned to look at him. "He didn't sleep with me. That is to say, he did, but it was on separate cots, in separate rooms."

Martha's mind drifted back to a conversation she'd had that morning when Jason had come over to Birds 'n' Beans. Sitting at the counter, sipping a cup of coffee, he'd pushed his baseball cap back on his head.

"Well, roomie, I guess this is goodbye," he said.

"What do you mean?" Martha had asked.

"It's time for me to leave the nest."

"Ha-ha, you're hardly a helpless hatchling."

"Cheep! Cheep! Seriously, though," he said, "I need to get things sorted out at my parents' house. I went over yesterday. The power's back on and it's a fine place for me to stay while my shop is repaired. I can even operate some of my already-booked trips from there so I don't lose every bit of income I was counting on for December. I can get the house ready for sale, so staying there works out on multiple levels."

Martha felt herself on the verge of blurting, "No! Stay here," but as much as she'd enjoyed the sense of another human in the vicinity when she closed her eyes at night, she couldn't deny him this opportunity to move past his painful childhood, hopefully once and for all.

She took a deep breath and forced herself back into the moment. She was here with Teddy, not Jason. Opening her mouth to continue, she snapped it shut when Teddy placed his index finger in front of his lips. She stopped allowing her mind to drift and waited.

"I'm just glad you're OK," he repeated.

"How are things going with the case?" she asked, not sure how much he'd be able to say, but curious anyway.

Teddy gave a long exhale. "It's quite a story, and it took an unexpected turn just before I headed over here."

Martha sat up straighter. "How so?"

"I'm going to tell you, because I'm pretty sure this will come out soon, but I'd appreciate you not telling anyone for a couple more days." Martha put her thumb and index finger together and drew an invisible zipper across her lips. "We just got a call from the medical examiner in Knoxville. Seems that Marshall was likely already dead when Frieda shot him."

"What? What do you mean?" Martha asked as he studied her face.

"The reason there was so little blood around his body was that it had already stopped circulating before he was shot. It's likely he'd frozen to death before she put the bullet into him."

"So... he wasn't murdered?" Martha asked, trying to piece together the implications of this new information.

"That's one the District Attorney will need to figure out, but from where I'm sitting, Tanner killed the man through negligence, then Frieda tried to kill him with a bullet. What a way to go."

"Oh, Teddy." Martha closed her eyes, trying to take in the latest twist of the week's horrible saga. "What happens now?"

"What happens now is I have to get back to the station," Teddy said as he rose and kissed her cheek. "See you tomorrow, I hope." With that, he strode back into the darkness.

Penny looked up at Martha and they sat quietly for a few minutes.

"Well, girl, turns out this village isn't exactly the quiet mountain hideaway I thought it might be. But what do you say we keep giving Riley Creek a go? Maybe we can still figure out our place here."

Penny sat up and copied Teddy, kissing Martha's cheek. Martha put an arm around the schnauzer and the two of them stayed there, warm in each other's company, looking out into the night and wondering what tomorrow would bring.

If you enjoyed Martha and Penny's adventures, be sure to check out the next book in the Riley Creek Cozy Mystery Series, *Maps, Mockingbirds, and Misdeeds*!

Get your claws on more bird and coffee-related content by signing up for my newsletter at **marylucal.com**. You'll get access to:

- Sneak peeks at upcoming books
- Fun and easy recipes (if I can make them anyone can!)
- Bird-y trivia
- Exclusive content

To learn more about the very non-fictional decline in wild bird populations that Ana mentioned, start here:

HTTPS://WWW.BIRDS.CORNELL.edu/home/bring-birds-back

About the Author

Mary Lucal is happy to be putting her English and Women's Studies double major to use, creating flawed yet brave female sleuths who get a little help from Mother Nature to solve mysteries.

Mary is the author of the Riley Creek Cozy Mystery Series, including *Hiking Sticks, Hawks, and Homicide* and *Binoculars, Blue Jays, and Bloodshed.*

A university administrator by day, Mary resides in Tennessee and spends her free time birding, hiking, camping, biking, or gardening.

www.ingramcontent.com/pod-product-compliance
Lightning Source LLC
Chambersburg PA
CBHW031531310726
48971CB00008B/2432